Praise for *The Invis*

"Doubinsky's narrative, broken up into segments represented by the Major Arcana of the tarot, is brisk, and he ably presents his near-future world of city-states moving in and out of cold and hot wars. . . . a fine installment in the series as a whole."
—Booklist

"In Seb Doubinsky's dystopian novel *The Invisible*, politics are the only game in town. . . . Brief, staccato chapters sparkle with surprising twists. . . . Though Georg finally realizes that he's just another bear in the circus, he is content with his role. In the stark novel, life is smothered by a mutually parasitic culture."
—Foreword Reviews

"In text that flares, sizzles, hisses and crackles, things are not what they seem in a fiction that exists in a moment. . . . Doubinsky's *The Invisible* is a titillating speculative thriller that is everything you expect and more."
—Aurealis Magazine

"The author's well-paced storytelling drew me deep into the dystopian city-state of New Babylon, a world which, with its political corruption, power struggles, economic uncertainty and the threat from a powerful new drug, felt all too recognizably topical!"
—Linda Hepworth, NB Magazine (5 stars)

"Seb Doubinsky's *The Invisible* is proof positive that often less is more—its chapters neat, sharp tiles in a complex mosaic. It reminded of Simenon and Lem for noir and the politics of a dystopian hierarchy, and reminded of Doubinsky in its brushes with Egyptian mythologies and a weird untethered experience for the reader. Even if this is your first foray into the City-States Cycle, it's as good an entry point as any. Fascinating structure, cool clear prose."
—Jeffrey Ford, author of *Out Of Body* and *The Best Of Jeffrey Ford*

"*The Invisible* is an all-consuming, hard-boiled mystery: terrifically told, unexpectedly poetic, and refreshingly non-apologetic."
—Viken Berberian, author of *The Cyclist* and *The Structure Is Rotten, Comrade*

"While politicians on the right spew hate, those on the left are the puppets of insidious corporations, and together they uphold a system that murders artists and rebels. But an honest whiskey-sipping cop shines a light on that which might offer a small dose of redemption: punk rock, trade unions, and slow-burning romantic love. Seb Doubinsky's *The Invisible* is a wry and tender novel, one that breathes fresh air into the tones of old-school noir, providing a balm for our absurd, terrifying times."
—Hirsh Sawhney, author of *South Haven*

"Beneath its neonoir plot about mysterious murders during a fraught presidential election, this sly and subversive page-turner offers radical ideas about the unseen workings of art, the politics of perception, and the ways subcultures can shift the social fabric in these perilous times."
—Jeff Jackson, author of *Destroy All Monsters*

"Just as *The Big Sleep* is guided by the imagery of the Grail myth, Seb Doubinsky's smoky, Chandleresque mystery follows a profane tarot into murder and heavy drugs, New Babylon's dark politics, and the Egyptian occult. Doubinsky's a grand master of terse episodes, tight rooms and close dialogue. His clean style and terrific sense of pacing are in the finest traditions of noir. Georg Ratner is part Bogart, and part something like Mad Men's Don Draper with punk rock tastes, a hardboiled investigator falling into mysticism, and a Faustian bargain. Add a wicked sense of irony to all this weird beauty, and you have a killer novel."
—James Reich, author of the *Song My Enemies Sing*

"Sebastian Doubinsky's *The Invisible* is dystopian fiction at its most 'mythical,' to paraphrase Georg Ratner, City Commissioner of New Babylon, who is trying to solve his ex-partner's murder and discover the source of a new reality-altering drug called Synth. Alternately melancholic and absurdist, *The Invisible* is both dire and whimsical, paranoid as early Thomas Pynchon, psychedelic as P.K. Dick and as full of wonder as anything by J.G. Ballard."
—J.S. Breukelaar, author of *Aletheia* and *Collision: Stories*

"What do a tweeting politician and the occult have in common? Seb Doubinsky's *The Invisible* staggers the world with a new offering that's part of Doubinsky's dystopian universe of the City-States series. *The Invisible* cascades at a spectacular pace with witty illustrated epigraphs on fools, magicians, priestesses, hierophants and more. The political thriller with its short, sharp style of bite-sized chapters whirls you into a metropolis that feeds on its ghosts."
—Eugen Bacon, author of *Claiming T-Mo*

"To confine *The Invisible* to a single genre belies its complexity. Part satire, part geopolitical commentary, part science fiction—and yes, absolutely, part noir—Doubinsky's latest is another mind-bending excursion into the fractured reality of his City-States; a world enough like our own to offer a terrifying clarity of vision, so different as to make us question the foundations of our reality."
—Kurt Baumeister, author of *Pax Americana*

"Doubinsky's dystopian detective novel reveals our greatest weapon against tyranny; at once gripping, beautiful, and meditative. A must read."
—Vincenzo Bilof, author of *The Violators, Dark Rising* and *The Profane*

"Questions, hints, and echoes float, fade and reappear as reality shifts little by little until nothing is what it seems. In a fog-bound city, a hapless bureaucrat investigates a murder, following a path like a Mobius strip between shifty political factions, heading for a fate for us all that may have already occurred. It's a lyrical, noir, ontological depth-charge that brings a primal fear with the truth, and a line from Yeats: 'what rough beast, it's hour come round at a last, slouches toward Bethlehem to be born?' This one will haunt you."
—Roy Freirich, author of *Deprivation* and *Winged Creatures*

"A poetic, smoke-wrapped puzzle box of a book that folds in on itself with each crisp turn of the page. Doubinsky writes like a chess master, shifting his pieces confidently around the board, always one step ahead of the reader. Excuse me while I read it again."
—Kyle Richardson, author of *Beast Heart* and *Wild Horse*

Also by Seb Doubinsky

The City-States Cycle

The Babylonian Trilogy
White City
The Song of Synth
Omega Gray
Absinth
Suan Ming
Missing Signal

Poetry

Mothballs: Quantum Poems
Zen and the Art of Poetry Maintenance
Spontaneous Combustions
Mountains
This Little Poem
Sketches

THE INVISIBLE

SEB DOUBINSKY

Meerkat Press
Atlanta

THE INVISIBLE. Copyright © 2020 by Seb Doubinsky.

All rights reserved. No part of this publication may be used, reproduced, distributed, or transmitted in any form or by any means without prior written permission from the publisher, except in the case of brief quotations embodied in critical reviews and certain other noncommercial uses permitted by copyright law. For information, contact Meerkat Press at *info@meerkatpress.com*.

ISBN-13 978-1-946154-27-9 (Paperback)
ISBN-13 978-1-946154-28-6 (eBook)

Library of Congress Control Number: 2020938686

This is a work of fiction. Names, characters, businesses, places, events and incidents are either the products of the author's imagination or used in a fictitious manner. Any resemblance to actual persons, living or dead, or actual events is purely coincidental.

Cover design & book design by Tricia Reeks

Printed in the United States of America

Published in the United States of America by
Meerkat Press, LLC, Atlanta, Georgia
www.meerkatpress.com

To Juan Carlos Suarez, Jerry Wilson and Antoni Casas Ros,
mis hermanos

In memoriam Lenora Lapidus, 1963–2019

"But tenderness, I discover, is the best memorial to tenderness."

—*Aldous Huxley.*

0/XXII. The Fool

The Fool: Creative inspiration. Leaving home for no reason whatsoever. A possibility of peace through ignorance. Stepping in dog shit.
Immunity against poison. Coming home for no reason whatsoever.

1

City Commissioner Georg Ratner looked out the large window of his new office, taking in the breathtaking view of the city. New Babylon sparkled in the mid-November morning. The sky was still black, although a thin gray stripe in the east indicated the imminent rise of a pale sun.

"Is everything okay, sir?"

Ratner glanced at the large designer desk, the designer leather armchair, the designer wastebasket, the designer bookshelves, his personal water fountain and nodded.

"Everything's fine," he grunted. "Everything's fine. I just need an ashtray."

"Yes, of course."

Ratner smiled with gratitude at his new secretary, Mrs. Gardiner. She smiled back.

She was a middle-aged woman who could have been anything between forty-five and sixty-five, as she had almost no wrinkles and her hair was died a reddish brown. Good-looking too, although that had nothing to do with anything. Ratner hated those automatic thoughts whenever they popped up. He was neither a sexist, nor a satyr. But sometimes his sense of observation collided with obsolete social constructions. Or rather—with constructions that should be obsolete.

"Mr. Klein smoked too. The pipe," she added.

Ratner nodded. He was replacing a dead man, who had the paradoxical reputation of being both extremely corrupt and extremely efficient. It would be hard to live up to his level.

"I smoke cigarettes," Ratner said. "And cigars, once in a while. I hope you don't mind."

Mrs. Gardiner tugged at her black turtleneck.

"I smoke too," she explained. "Oh, and Mr. Klein had a minibar installed while he was in office. I mean, it's a minifridge. You can put in whatever you want, of course. Water, for example. It's in the basement at the moment. I can ask Eric to bring it back for you."

Ratner didn't know if she was making things up, but her tone seemed hopeful.

"Yes," he said. "That would be very nice."

Once Mrs. Gardiner had left, the new city commissioner walked to his desk and sat in the designer armchair. It was more comfortable than he had imagined.

2

Ratner was sitting in a dead man's chair, although, technically, his predecessor had never used it. The office had been completely redone to welcome him. There was a small framed black-and-white picture hanging on a wall, showing the way the office looked before (old-style and cozy)—a clipping from the *New Babylonian Post* from a few years back. Klein stood behind his desk, surrounded by Maggie Delgado, the current president, Jack Tchebick, the current mayor, and Jim Flowers, the current DA—the last two, the same team that had pushed Ratner all the way to the top.

Ratner had only done his job correctly, though. No corruption, in the traditional sense of the word, at least. Sure, a couple of small favors here and there. But never anything serious, nor criminal. Parking tickets, desk jobs, transfers. That sort of thing. And catching criminals. That got him a reputation and respect among the colleagues. That's what Ratner wanted to believe. Respect. It was a heavy word—much heavier than "responsibilities" or even "power." Respect opened very door, even in the criminal world. He looked for his cigarettes in the pocket of his jacket, then remembered there weren't any ashtrays in the office. A plastic cup from the water fountain would do. Creative thinking. Another of his *forte*. The smoke filled his lungs like a welcome lethal gas.

3

Ratner had barely sat down again behind the large desk when the phone rang. "Yes?"

"You haven't forgotten about the press conference tonight?"

He recognized Mayor Tchebick's voice. No need for introductions. "No, of course not."

"You wrote your speech?"

Ratner cringed. "Yes," he lied.

"It would be a good thing if you showed it to Mrs. Gardiner. She excels in editing."

"Sure."

"See you tonight, then."

The mayor hung up without waiting for an answer. Ratner looked at the pile of files already towering on his desk. As if he had time to write a speech. He sighed and buzzed Mrs. Gardiner.

4

Ratner had hesitated for a few days before accepting the promotion. Actually, he hadn't even told Laura about the offer initially. When he finally did, he had already made up his mind.

"But you hate politics," she had rightly said.

He had taken her to a new Italian restaurant on the corner of their street. He wanted to be out of their apartment to announce the news. Both for a celebration and an excuse.

"I know," he had said, pouring more wine into her glass. "But I hate Thomsen even more."

Thomsen was the northern district commissioner. In Ratner's eyes, he symbolized everything he despised: incompetence, hunger for power, backstabbing and an excellent network of high-ranking incompetents, like Thomsen himself.

"That's still politics," Laura said. "In a good way."

She smiled and raised her glass to her lips. In the candlelight her mouth appeared dark red. Ratner thought of cherries in the spring.

"Jim practically begged me to accept," he explained. "And Tchebick is afraid of Thomsen. For obvious reasons."

Laura nodded. She knew everything about the city's murky secrets. Ratner confided in her because he trusted her with all the soul he had left.

"So I accepted," he concluded.

"Good," Laura said. "But don't come crying when the walls fall down. Because you know they always do in the end."

5

But don't come crying when the walls fall down. Because you know they always do in the end. Laura's encouraging words echoed in his mind as Mrs. Gardiner stepped in.

"Yes?" she asked.

"I was wondering if you got hold of that ashtray I required?"

Mrs. Gardiner lifted her hand in a blessing gesture, her index pointed at the ceiling. "I knew I had forgotten something. I'll be right back."

Ratner smiled as she shut the door behind her, and he picked up the first file on the pile.

I. THE MAGICIAN

The Magician: Things are not what they seem. A headache, a passing buzz, a slight confusion. Watch the other hand. The secret is that there is no secret. Only technique. But the technique is a secret. Make-believe. Remember to clean the table after the party.

1

Tchebick and Flowers were standing in the mayor's crowded office, both smoking—Flowers, a cigarette; the mayor, a short fat cigar from some sunny and corrupt island.

"Ah, Ratner!" Tchebick shouted over the heads and the hubbub as he noticed the city commissioner. "Come here."

A few heads turned as Ratner squeezed through a wall of shoulders and male cologne. He only distinguished two feminine figures in the crowd, both spin doctors. The mayor grabbed the newly appointed city commissioner's arm and dragged him closer.

"You brought your speech, right? Hope it's not too long. Don't forget to mention the new law."

Flowers nodded at the mayor's words, but Ratner knew it was more politeness than acquiescence. The two men had been side by side for a long time, but deep rifts cracked beneath the surface of their collaboration. Tchebick was a bulldozer, while Flowers—maybe because of his surname—liked more subtle approaches, especially when fighting, or at least tackling crime. Their career in corruption also differed: where Flowers discreetly did favors to friends and friends of friends, Tchebick's connections shoveled millions into his offshore accounts. Morals was a word that had been erased a long time ago from New Babylon politics, and Ratner himself wasn't even sure what it really meant anymore.

"The new law" was getting political assassination back on the serious crime list. For about twenty years, assassination had been legal if the silent partner had an official contract with one of the seventeen approved assassination corporations in the city. The only exceptions on the list, until now, were cops and Justice Department officials. The idea was to take some pressure off the shoulders of the overworked police department and, at the same time, make a profit by taxing heavily these contracts.

Unfortunately, recent events had changed the general consensus as some terrorist attacks had been conducted within this legal frame. The double assassination of the New Moscow and Chinese Alliance ambassadors had caused huge diplomatic damage, and things had to be controlled again. The new law, therefore, excluded politically motivated murder from the legal list.

Flowers warmly tapped Ratner's shoulder and handed him a drink. Ratner took a sip. Warm champagne. Perfect drink for the occasion.

2

"Great speech, Ratner," Tchebick said once the reporters had left the communication room. "Short, precise. Everything I like. I could recognize Mrs. Gardiner's hand anywhere."

He winked at the city commissioner, who answered with a thin smile. Ratner's hand crushed the list of errands he had in his pocket, and which he had pretended to read from during the press conference.

3

Laura was watching TV as he walked into their apartment. She hadn't turned on the light in the sitting room, and her face shone like a colorful wall.

"How did it go?" she asked while he hung his jacket in the small hallway.

He took his pack of cigarettes out and sat down next to her. The scent from her hair reached his nostrils. Perfume, sweat and tobacco. Magic.

She helped herself to one of his cigarettes, sticking it between her lips as he looked for a lighter in the pocket of his pants. Like him, she smoked nonfilter.

"It went," he answered, staring absent-mindedly at the film she was watching.

A woman was running away from a blond young man in an English garden. The man didn't follow her and just stayed where he was, perplexed. He was holding a camera. They looked European, from the sixties. An old film.

"What are you watching?"

"*Blow up*. Antonioni. I don't understand anything, but I was too tired to switch. Was Thomsen there?"

"No. Of course not."

He suddenly felt like a whisky. Every time Thomsen's name came up, he felt like a stiff drink. Pavlovian reflex. Grunting, he stood up.

"And how was your day?" he shouted from the kitchen while pouring some whisky into a large glass. He added two ice cubes and a little water.

"Fine," Laura answered as he sat down again next to her.

She worked as a special education teacher in a school for special needs children. "Nobody tried to strangle anybody else today."

Some of the kids were becoming violent as puberty approached. They sometimes became dangerous, but to Laura it had become routine.

Ratner took a long sip of his whisky and put a hand on her thigh. Violence linked them in a strange way, he thought, then took another sip to chase that thought away.

4

Laura was asleep, a warm and hilly landscape next to him. His thoughts were retracing some of the events of the day: the new office, the interview, the discussion with Tchebick and Flowers, the pile of files on his office. Nothing was chronological, only bits and fragments of conversations and situations.

Ratner wondered if the weird construction of the sixties film he had watched with Laura had influenced his brain. And what a strange movie it was: a man witnesses what he thinks is a murder, what is *obviously* a murder, but cannot prove it and gives up. Ratner, as a cop, couldn't accept this, and yet it made perfect sense. It was the very definition of a "perfect murder." Something all can see, but none can prove. A magical trick of the highest level, an undeniable fact turning into an illusion. The city commissioner felt the synapses of his brain flare and crackle. *It was only a fiction*, he told himself. *The perfect murder doesn't exist. Only perfect good luck combined with a bad investigation.*

II. THE HIGH PRIESTESS

The High Priestess: Love is in the air. The desire of gardening. Feeling superstitious. The possibility of understanding something not yet asked. A blowjob. Something divine.

1

City Commissioner Georg Ratner signed the tenth search warrant of the day and decided it was time for a cigarette. He stood up and stretched, looking with disgust at the pile of papers and files he had to look at for the rest of the afternoon.

Lighting up a cigarette, he contemplated the bleak skyline that he somehow loved so much. New Babylon was a mythical place, filled with the ghosts of famous writers, artists, actors, wannabes, dead or alive. This metropolis had killed more than any disease; it had a kiss of death that no one could resist. That's probably why the river running in its middle, separating the city in two almost equal halves, like a liquid scar, had been called the Styx. The legend said that the very first colonists had been awed by the size of that large, dark stretch of water, but Ratner thought that the founding fathers must have had a prophet among them, maybe even the Pythia, disguised as an old hag, who had whispered the name in their ears.

Yes, indeed, New Babylon was a huge cemetery, a mausoleum of epic proportions and yet . . . yet it was also very much alive. Like plants ingest carbon monoxide and breathe back oxygen, Babylon fed on its ghosts to breathe back life. Nothing seemed to disappear forever here—it remained, hovering in between the sound of the cars' horns, the light of the sunset reflected in the shop windows and the shadows of the passersby, hurrying home after work.

Ratner's thoughts moved to Barbara, his first wife, who had drifted in a coma for years before finally reaching the other side. She was still here for him, a whiff of perfume, a distant laughter, a flickering thought. Her photo was next to Laura's on his desk—her colors slightly faded, of course. He had met Laura during Barbara's coma, and she had supported him emotionally throughout the long, endless tunnel of his wife's agony. Ratner hadn't felt any remorse meeting Laura; she had appeared like a tiny flower at the end of a very long winter. It hadn't been betrayal, it had been hope.

Today, he thought of Barbara side by side with Nūt, the Egyptian goddess of night Ratner loved so much. In his dreams, they would be sometimes sitting next to each other, like old friends. Old friends from the other side. Those who never betrayed you or let you down.

2

"City Commissioner, someone would like to see you."

Ratner was startled by the voice on the speaker. He put down the file he was reading and stooped toward the built-in microphone. "Who is it?"

He heard Mrs. Gardiner ask the visitor his name but didn't get the distant muffled answer.

"Captain Jesse Valentino, sir. From the Finance Division," Mrs. Gardiner dutifully relayed.

Ratner smiled. Jesse Valentino! So many memories whirled in the city commissioner's mind. They had worked together as partners in the Homicide Department, years ago. Valentino had just come out of the Academy and Ratner had been his mentor, teaching him the tricks of the trade.

They had been together on the Cartoon Killer case, which had pushed them under the media's spotlight—which they had both hated with equal passion. The self-proclaimed "Cartoon Killer" was a serial killer who, like Jack the Ripper, butchered prostitutes in order to gain fame. He actually wore cartoon character costumes and took selfies of himself next to the mutilated bodies, which he sent to the media.

He had also sent Ratner many personal notes, as a tribute to the Ripper's *modus operandi* with Scotland Yard. He and Jesse had put an end to his evil deeds on live TV and had become "heroes" overnight. (He had actually never completely forgiven his old friend, journalist Sheryl Boncoeur for her stunt of filming him while he shot down the killer, the only time he had ever used his gun.) Two years later, Valentino had decided to switch to the Finance Division, "to catch the real criminals," he had said.

Valentino had always been an idealist, and Ratner saw himself as a pessimist-realist, although Laura called him a pessimist-pessimist. Fighting crime, for Valentino, had the value of a religious crusade. He remembered the young officer as over-empathetic, often crying at crime scenes or being depressed for days. He also wrote poetry and had published a collection, *Red & Blue*, or something like that, a few years back. Ratner had a signed copy lying somewhere at home. He had actually liked some of them. A cop and a poet. Ratner smiled again.

"Sure, let him in," Ratner said, wondering how his old partner looked now, as one is always curious about the effects of age.

3

Valentino hadn't changed so much over the years. It was both surprising and a little scary. He had exactly the same toothpaste-commercial smile and shining deep-blue eyes that Ratner remembered. The guy could have easily chosen a career as a crook, a priest or a politician, and made it to the top. Unfortunately honesty usually was a career-stopper in New Babylon and Ratner would have been surprised if Valentino ever became commissioner. He welcomed the extended hand, which crushed his enthusiastically.

"Wonderful seeing you again, Georg," Valentino said, sitting down across Ratner. "And congratulations on the new job! You're definitely the best for the part!"

"Not everyone agrees with you," the city commissioner grumbled, feeling somewhat flattered in spite of himself. "What brings you here?"

Valentino joined his hands over the surface of the desk, frowning. Ratner thought for an embarrassing second he was going to pray.

"I need support from someone I can trust," Valentino said.

Ratner nodded, waiting for more.

"I need a search warrant, but my direct superior has denied me his authorization."

"Really? Why?"

"He hasn't told me directly but hinted at pressures from above."

"Who is in charge of your district?"

Valentino sighed and looked straight at the commissioner. His blue eyes seemed to be evaluating Ratner.

"Thomsen," he finally said. "I don't trust him."

"Ah," Ratner said, noncommittally.

"I know I shouldn't be saying that."

Ratner kept quiet. Valentino understood the unspoken support.

"But I think you know what I mean."

Ratner leaned back in his chair. He felt like a cigarette. He had just started his new job and the walls were already threatening to fall on him. Laura had been right. As usual.

"Tell me what you need this warrant for."

"Well, I'm investigating this company, Green Star—it's a very small company, specialized in fair-trade imports. Coffee, mainly. They work with hip coffee shops, a few restaurants, some cafeterias, one or two corporations. They're doing alright and their gross income has been very stable. Nothing suspicious there. But I got a tip—"

"Let me guess: they also import drugs." Ratner interrupted.

Valentino smiled and shook his head. "No, it's not that simple. If you check them on the web, you won't see anything suspicious. The owner, Sam Rosen, is clean, or at least seems to be. I would have never found anything suspect if I hadn't received a tip."

Ratner was curious now. "What was the tip about?"

"It was a forwarded email. It was from Sam Rosen, the CEO, to Helena Gonzalez."

"*The* Helena Gonzalez?"

Valentino nodded. "Herself."

Ratner pursed his lips. Gonzalez was one of the most powerful lawyers of New Babylon, who represented most of the city's multinational corporations. It was rumored she had ties to foreign powers—namely New Moscow and the Chinese Alliance—as well as the underworld. Nothing had ever been proven, and she seemed invulnerable. She was also a good friend and adviser to Ted Rust, the presidential candidate running against Maggie Delgado in the upcoming election.

"And what was this email about?" Ratner asked.

Valentino unfolded a printed page he had extracted from the pocket of his jacket and handed it to the city commissioner.

Rosen was explaining that they had run into some unexpected problems, and he was asking Gonzalez if she could help him with "damage control," to which she answered she would see what could be done.

"Damage control? What did he mean by that? I thought you told me it was a very low-key company. Did anybody find GMOs in their coffee beans?"

Valentino shrugged. "I had no idea until I saw this in the paper a week later."

This time he handed Ratner an article clipped from the *Babylonian Times*, dated three weeks ago. Ratner glanced at the title. "Green Star Executive Found Dead in a Hotel Room." The victim, a certain John Harding, had suffocated himself in what appeared to be an autoerotic game.

"A classic," Ratner sighed. "Who was in charge of the investigation?"

"Northern District Commissioner Thomsen."

"I see." Ratner's mind raced. "And you don't think it was an accident?" he asked Valentino.

"I don't know. I tried to get my hands on the autopsy report, but I was told it was missing. 'Probably misplaced,' they said."

"Yeah, it happens," Ratner said, unconvinced.

"Sure."

Ratner drummed his fingers on his desk. "And why do you think this Harding sent you the email in the first place?" Ratner asked.

"No idea," Valentino said. "Now it looks like it was a cry for help or something."

Ratner changed position in his chair. "Hierarchically, I am over Thomsen," he finally said.

Valentino nodded. "That's why I came to see you."

"But this implies that you do not trust him even though he is the head of your district. If nothing comes out of this, you might lose your job. And I will need a good lawyer too."

Just hired, already in trouble, Ratner thought.

"I know," Valentino said. "You can say no. I will understand."

"What do you want the search warrant for?"

"To get into Green Star's office and see if I can put my hands on Harding's work computer. It wasn't at his home; I checked with the detectives in charge of the investigation of his suicide. I want to check his emails, if anything was erased, that kind of thing. I can't have Thomsen warn them, if he's not clean."

Ratner nodded. He knew the guy had ambition and would sell his mother to organ traffickers for a promotion, but he hadn't imagined him linked to a possible murder.

"Give me the warrant, but you have to promise me that you will keep a very low profile. Officially, stick to the possible murder investigation. Say his bank account had some discrepancies, or whatever. Nothing else. And see if you find anything on Thomsen and Gonzalez, while you're at it. Keep me in the loop. But discreetly."

"My intention from the start," Valentino said, his blue eyes burning earnest holes into Ratner's as he handed him the paperwork.

The guy could be too intense sometimes, the city commissioner thought. He wondered if Valentino had a partner. In a sexual sense, he meant.

"How's life, apart from that? It's been a long time!" he asked as he signed the warrant.

"Fine, thanks."

"Wife? Partner? Children?"

Valentino smiled as he took the signed papers. "No, unfortunately not. Too busy, I'm afraid."

"And the poetry?"

"Still writing, thank you. I have a new collection coming out soon. Can't stop writing. It's like a curse, you know."

The city commissioner smiled and shook his hand. Valentino closed the door behind him, and Ratner stared into empty space for a few seconds. It had been good to see his old partner, but he also wondered if it had been *a good thing*.

III. THE EMPRESS

The Empress: An interview. A walk in a forest. A good harvest. A box of condoms. A good friend one oversees. Ruling over one's own house or apartment. The possibility of applied strength.

1

"Have you thought about your sponsors?" Mayor Tchebick asked Ratner after the weekly morning briefing.

Everybody had left except for the city commissioner and the DA, Jim Flowers.

"No, not really. I have to speak to my wife. She can be very touchy about these things."

In order to fight against corruption, the Delgado government had passed a law which obliged all high-ranking officials to declare sponsors from an official list. The higher you were, the longer the list and the slots available. As city commissioner, Ratner had two slots. The president thirty-five. If lobbying was officially forbidden, this law still allowed private funds to pour into political parties' pockets, but in a more "transparent" way.

"I understand," Jim Flowers said.

"Who cares about what the wives think?" Tchebick snorted. "Just tell her I imposed them on you. She will hate me, not you. I don't mind."

"I can't do that," Ratner replied, although he thought it wasn't so bad an idea.

"I am actually surprised she let you accept the position, Georg," Flowers interjected. "Laura is the true anarchist!"

Flowers had met Laura a couple of times at receptions and private dinners where she had, of course, stated her clear-cut political and social opinions.

"Well, in any case, Bolshevik wife or not, I need your documents by tomorrow," Tchebick said. "And Flowers, we need to talk about that Synth problem, if you have five minutes."

Ratner took his leave, knowing well what the two men were about to discuss. "Synth" was a new drug that had recently reached New Babylon, becoming an instant hit like LSD in the late sixties. It supposedly opened up alternate realities and even gave the users the illusion of having supernatural powers like telepathy, invisibility and telekinesis, according to tabloids.

Nothing new here, except that the elections were coming up and presidential candidate Rust was using it full blast in his campaign, accusing the Delgado administration of closing their eyes on the problem. What Tchebick and Flowers would talk about was pure politics, and nothing pragmatic. *As usual*, the city commissioner thought to himself while waiting for the elevator. He refrained from sighing as the doors opened.

2

"Mrs. Gardiner, would you bring me the list of the official city commissioner sponsors, please?" Ratner buzzed the secretary, while lighting a cigarette.

He was seated in his comfortable armchair, and felt like a whisky. On the rocks, in a large glass, with some nice industrial jazz playing in the background. The mirage of comfort.

"There you go, sir," Mrs. Gardiner said, handing him two A4 pages. "They're indexed both by names and by domain."

Ratner looked with surprise at the pages. "I sincerely thought it would be longer," he said.

"It's written in very small print," the secretary explained. "Good reading."

3

In the car, driving home, Ratner thought about the two sponsors he had chosen. One was the New Babylon Tobacco Company and the other the New Babylon Spirits Import. At least these two companies couldn't be accused of hiding their purpose, which was to kill their consumers. Death was the only card they dealt, and it seemed fitting for a city commissioner. He smiled at his own cynicism as the light turned red. He stopped and looked at the still traffic around him, glinting softly in the November dark. Laura was going to have a fit.

4

Laura was in the shower when he walked into the apartment.

"I'm home," he yelled, like in a bad comedy.

"Okay!" she yelled back, her voice muffled by the water and the closed door.

Ratner took off his jacket and walked into the kitchen, where he grabbed a glass and some ice cubes from the freezer. He poured himself that double whisky he had been dreaming of since the morning and dropped on the leather couch, letting out a grunt of satisfaction.

Laura appeared, wearing what appeared to be a set of fresh clothes and smelling of perfume. Her wet hair was tucked under a towel shaped in a turban.

"I'm not staying, I have this dinner with my colleagues I told you about," she said disappearing into the bedroom.

Ratner nodded. He didn't remember, of course.

"How was your meeting, by the way?"

He took a long sip of his drink to clear his voice. Here he was, one of the most powerful civil figures in New Babylon, afraid of his wife's opinion.

"Fine, fine. I had to pick up my two official sponsors," he said, lowering his voice in the second part of the sentence.

"Oh yeah? Who did you choose?" Laura asked, walking out again with a hairdryer in her hand. She walked back into the bathroom. The dryer began to howl.

"I chose the New Babylon Tobacco Company and the New Babylon Spirits Import."

"What?"

He repeated it, louder.

The howling ceased. Laura stuck her head out. "Are you serious?"

Ratner shrugged, nodded and took refuge behind the ice cubes in his glass. Laura burst into a laughter.

"But that's a great idea! Terrific! I *love* it!"

"You really mean it?" he asked, surprised.

"Of course! At least, you're honest. Not like those bastards hiding their corruption and cynicism behind charities. You're claiming your Philip Marlowe and Lew Archer heritage. I love it!"

She came over to the couch and gave him a resounding kiss on the mouth. He felt her wet hair fall on his face like a Chinese pearl-curtain. It tingled and smelled good.

"You're the bestest," she said.

"So are you," Ratner whispered.

"I know."

Winking, Laura eloped to the bathroom again. The electrical howling resumed. Ratner took a sip of his whisky. Philip Marlowe and Lew Archer. He liked that. He liked that very, very much.

IV. THE EMPEROR

The Emperor: A visit to the barber's. Some things better left unsaid. Eating an apple. A desire to see mountains. A paper crown. Unnecessary wrinkles.

1

Ratner had always hated figures, although he had the strongest respect for mathematics. To him, they were two distinct entities, like religions and gods. The first were power constructs, the latter pure mystery.

He glanced one last time at the newest provisional budget spreadsheet lying on his desk and decided it was time for a well-deserved break. He had already wasted the entire morning trying to figure things out, with the blessed help of Mrs. Gardiner, and still felt like he understood as little as before.

He took a cigarette out of its package and lit it while checking his emails. One caught his attention. It was from Jesse Valentino. It had been a week since his old pard had visited him, and Ratner wondered if Jesse had already collected some info. He opened it, but there was just a short message and a link.

"Hello Georg! It was nice to see you. Here is the link to my upcoming collection."

The city commissioner clicked on the link. A fine cover appeared, with a nice illustration. It was titled *Verses from the Dark Side.*

Shitty title, Ratner thought. The publisher was unknown to him, but then again, that wasn't really surprising. He seldom read poetry, and when he did, they were usually classics published through well-established presses.

Taking a long drag of his cigarette, he told himself to remember to preorder it when he got home. Poets were the unbeknownst saviors of the world: their utter powerlessness was a paradoxical glimmer of hope.

2

The phone rang and startled him. It was his office phone, and it very seldom rang. When it did, it was usually bad news.

"City Commissioner Ratner," he grumbled.

"Georg, Jim Flowers. You know—the DA," Flowers joked.

Ratner let out a polite laugh.

"I hope I'm not disturbing you."

"Not at all. I was looking at the budget figures."

"I hate this administrative bullshit," Flowers said. "Just sign and say the figures look good. No one's going to blame you for not doing a job that isn't your job. You're not an accountant, for God's sake. Fuck budget cuts and get us some personal accountants."

"Word," Ratner agreed.

It was always good to hear the boss support you. He regretted not recording this conversation. He could have used it as evidence if he ever fucked up.

"What can I do for you, Jim?" he added, hoping the answer would be "Nothing."

"I need to see you about that Synth problem, you know? Tchebick is getting his balls squeezed by Delgado, who is feeling Rust's breath on her neck. Can we meet somewhere?"

"Sure. When?"

"As soon as possible. Like today."

"Why not my office?"

"Because your office."

"Okay. I see."

Flowers was afraid his office could be bugged. Who knew? Even Mrs. Gardiner could be a spy, working for Rust. The man had no scruples, it was public knowledge. Hell, he even bragged about it in the media all the time. "They play dirty, I'll play dirtier." Flowers might be right to be paranoid.

"There is a French-style café at the corner of Lermontov and Sixth Avenue. I can be there in thirty minutes," said Ratner.

"OK. See you."

Ratner looked at the spreadsheet one last time and buzzed Mrs. Gardiner. "I did the final check. All clear."

Fuck them, he thought, *and the accountants they rode in on.*

3

It was mid-afternoon and Le Robespierre Café was half-empty. Ratner scanned the tables, but Flowers hadn't arrived yet. The bartender nodded at the city commissioner, who nodded back. Ratner liked this place. He felt at home. Le Robespierre was a cult punk-rock bar, with a jukebox filled with great tunes and the beer was cheap. The whole place looked like a dirty rock 'n' roll saloon, with worn leather booths, wobbly inscribed tables and creaky chairs. There was a small resin model of a guillotine and a plaster bust of the French Revolutionary himself sitting high on a shelf behind the bar. The walls were covered with vintage concert posters and French Revolutionary leaflet reproductions.

Ratner ordered a pint of Guinness at the bar. He always felt relaxed here. It was his cave, his hiding place, when he wanted to have a good time and be left alone. This is the way Ratner remembered his youth, before he decided to become a cop. He sometimes took Laura, as well as his closest friends, like the journalist Sheryl Boncoeur or the established but controversial writer Lee Jones. But he mostly went alone, to meet some of the regulars there. No questions asked, fragments of life shared and moaned upon, and good, sincere laughter. And, of course, the occasional display of new tattoos. Sitting down in an empty booth facing the door, he wondered if Flowers knew about this place. Probably not. As most people of power did, Flowers only liked mainstream nonthreatening stuff. What he considered acceptable "punk" was Bob Dylan turning electric. The rest was just noise for uneducated kids. Who would probably end up in jail. *Or as city commissioners*, Ratner thought, with a smile.

4

"Ah, Georg!" Flowers said, as he entered the bar and spotted Ratner sitting behind his pint of stout. Ratner noticed with some amusement the surprised look on the DA's face as he joined him.

"Quite a joint," Flowers exclaimed, sitting down. "What are you drinking?"

"Guinness. It's good for you," Ratner said, quoting the Irish beer's famous motto.

"Probably," Flowers agreed, obviously not getting the reference and looking for a waitress to take his order.

"You've got to order at the bar," Ratner explained.

"Ah, yes, of course."

Somebody put the Sex Pistols "I did you no wrong" on the jukebox while Flowers was coming back, carefully carrying a half pint of IPA filled to the rim.

"I never imagined you liking this kind of place."

Ratner shrugged. "Reminds me of my childhood," he joked. "So, what's the big hush-hush about?"

Flowers took a sip of his hipster ale. A thin line of foam remained on his upper lip, looking like an old gentleman's mustache. He licked it off absent-mindedly and darted a nervous glance at the scarce patrons.

"Don't worry," Ratner said. "They're not interested. Unless you're selling."

"Actually, that's what I wanted to talk to you about. That drug . . . Synth, or whatever they're calling it. It's making Tchebick and Delgado very, very nervous."

"I can imagine that," the city commissioner said, diplomatically.

"Yeah. they're flipping like crazy, now that the story has hit the media big time. Rust is using it in his campaign and it's working, of course. He's only two clicks behind now."

"So . . . what do you . . . they . . . want me to do?"

Flowers took another nervous sip. With his dark blue suit and crazy colored tie, he was flashing all the bad signals in this joint, Ratner mused. The bartender would surely ask about him later. They all knew here who Ratner was, of course, but he was considered a familiar, a protective entity. "That guy, Flowers, though . . ." Ratner smiled to himself as he imagined the later conversation.

"I want you to step out in the spotlights and say you're personally going to take care of this Synth problem. That you're promising to do something about it. Personally."

Ratner tasted his Guinness. Just as bitter as it should be. "You said "personally" twice. I guess that's the important part."

Flowers nodded.

"If I understand correctly, you—or they—want me to jeopardize my budding city commissioner career from the start by promising *personally* something you and I know I can never achieve. Is it your idea or are you the messenger I am supposed to shoot?"

Flowers smiled nervously. "Well, you know . . . officially, it's my idea. They insisted on it. *My* idea. But I knew you wouldn't buy it."

Ratner nodded and remained silent for a few seconds. "What's in it for me?"

"I thought you were untouchable."

The city commissioner stretched his arms, making his knuckles crack. "Who says I'm not? Maybe I just want to hear, that's all."

"Your job will be guaranteed for the whole new term if Delgado gets elected. No matter what."

Ratner turned his head and let his eyes wander on the alcohol shelf behind the bar. "Sounds like a devil's deal. I am really selling my soul here."

Flowers sighed. "I know, I know. But look at it from another angle. We all agree that Delgado isn't perfect, that the Purple Party isn't as clean as it claims to be, but imagine Rust winning the next election. What will happen? Corruption, nepotism and aggressive foreign politics will replace—"

"The corrupted, nepotistic and aggressive politics we know now?" Ratner interrupted, with a wry smile. "But at least Delgado's not surfing on xenophobia, I'll give you that."

"Exactly," Flowers said, glad there was *something* that made Ratner tick. "The Blue Party has become a nest of bigoted and racist bastards."

"I forgot the bigotry, but yeah."

"So?" Flowers asked, his eyes pleading like a dog's that desperately wants to go out and pee.

"Can I think about it? It's not easy to accept becoming the sacrificial lamb for a bunch of corrupt politicians."

"The other side is worse. Much worse," Flowers said.

"You're right, that's why I have to think about it. Otherwise I would have said no from the start."

Ratner lifted his pint and they cheered, "No Fun" by the Stooges blasting from the jukebox.

5

He had promised Laura he'd pick her up at the school. After finding a space in the parking lot in front of the large building, he killed the engine but left the radio on. He let his thoughts follow the complex avant-garde jazz melodies, trying to avoid both the spreadsheets and the afternoon conversation with Flowers. When he recognized Laura coming out of the building, he turned the engine back on and she noticed the car. She waved and trotted toward him, illuminated by the headlights. He felt a warmth blossom behind his ribcage. That's exactly how he pictured her in his thoughts—illuminated. No, actually, not illuminated. Illuminating.

6

"Should we have a cat, you think?"

Ratner shrugged. This was a recurring question as they had no children—they had tried for a little while after Barbara's death, but to no avail—Laura sometimes imagined that a pet would be good company.

They were watching TV, some stupid foreign series about a serial murderer somewhere in Scandinavia. Everything was slow, beautiful and incredibly empty. The cops were particularly incompetent. Ratner wondered if this was pure fiction or a "realistic" rendition. The colleagues he had met from Viborg City on official visits hadn't impressed him much: they were cocky, stuffed, arrogant assholes. They came to New Babylon to learn something and pretended to know everything already. Which meant they went back as ignorant as they had come.

"We would have to find someone to take care of it when we go on vacation," he answered.

"You always say that, but we never go anywhere when we're on vacation."

Ratner shrugged and took a cigarette from the package on the coffee table. She was right, of course. During his vacation, Ratner liked to visit museums and go to the movies. He had traveled a lot when he was young but hated it now. Not discovering other places, but the travel part itself.

"We could change that, maybe," he said, lighting the cigarette. "Maybe take a trip during Easter vacation."

"I always wanted to see New Belleville," Laura said.

"I know. We could do that."

"Then a cat would definitely have to wait."

Ratner nodded, relieved. The decoy had worked for now. And maybe they could actually take a trip to New Belleville. Lee Jones considered moving there. The man hated everything, so it couldn't be that bad of a city. To visit, at least.

7

Ratner watched the news after the boring Scandinavian murder series. Laura was in the bathroom, brushing her teeth and getting ready to go to bed. Rust popped up in the "domestic" section, with his handsome face and perfect suit. You had to give it to him: he was younger, more fit and suntanned than President Delgado. He actually looked like a hero doctor in a 1960s soap opera, up to the whitened temples and the perfectly groomed jet-black hair. If votes were based on sole aesthetics, he would probably win by 99%.

"We have to get rid of the illegal scum that are infecting our city and stealing our good citizens' jobs," he said, his voice fading under the standing ovation.

Ratner took his cell phone out of his pants pocket and dialed Flowers.

V. THE HIEROPHANT

The Hierophant: What is obvious is what is hidden. The power of electricity. Watching Fritz Lang's *Metropolis*. Being admired by cretins. Misplacing your keys. Looking for answers in the eyes of a stranger.

1

Some arrests had been made. Minor dealers. Most of them art students, one with a rap sheet. Fifty Synth pills were found in a stash at their apartment. The police had used maximum brutality during the arrest, filmed by the invited media, triggering protests from human rights groups, attacked in their turn by Rust's supporters, accusing them of being anti-Babylonian. *Action and reaction*, Ratner thought as he stepped out of his office for the press conference. *Let's just hope this doesn't turn into a Hiroshima.*

2

Flowers called him immediately after the conference, as Ratner expected.

"Hey, Georg! Mayor Tchebick is next to me and he is very, very pleased to see you taking efficient steps against that Synth problem and endorsing full responsibility. He wants you to know you have his entire support on this. He will make a public statement later this evening."

After the call, Ratner lit a cigarette and reclined in his Nordic design leather armchair. He had accepted the charge to please his old friend Flowers and, deep down inside, to satisfy a secret ambition, but an old Taoist saying kept nagging him in the back of his head: "Gifts can be more dangerous than poisoned arrows." If he could apply it to the Flowers side of the situation, he just realized that it could also mean gifts to yourself. *You never stop learning,* he thought, and took another long drag, watching the gray spiraling column gradually fade as it rose toward the ceiling.

3

Although Ratner officially couldn't be directly in charge of a current investigation, the Synth case intrigued him. Where LSD had been a half-official drug created in government and corporate laboratories before going rogue, no one had a clue on Synth's provenance. Nobody could even come up with a stable formula, and none of the drug's recipes you could find for sale on the Deep Web seemed legit or even reliable. All official drug experts were baffled. The only technical element everybody agreed on was that it was a DNA based drug, and that it implied a highly skilled laboratory was required to produce it—all eyes turning to the Chinese Alliance and its best friend, the Democratic Monarchy of Samarqand.

Ratner had contacted Captain Eris Jordan, who supervised the Narcotics Department and who, by chance, was an old army pal. They had agreed to meet in her office, which was located in the new buildings on the other side of town. Sitting in the back of his official vehicle, Ratner observed the traffic and the passersby slowly fading in the early November sundown. Everything seemed gray and black. That's how the Romans pictured the Land of the Dead. A landscape of shadows. Who needed death when you had New Babylon in the late fall? Ratner smiled for himself and felt his love for his doomed, crooked and depressing city move up one notch.

4

"This is the list of the dealers we have arrested so far. Do you notice anything unusual?"

It was obviously a trick question. Ratner read and reread the names and listed occupations displayed on the computer screen. He could sense Captain Eris Jordan's hard glance evaluating him. She had owned a higher rank in the army and he was now her superior. Hence the test, probably. *Fair enough*, he thought as he concentrated on the rather short list. He couldn't see anything strange at first, then it struck him.

"They are all students, or have jobs."

"Exactly." Jordan nodded. Her flaming red hair was cut short, a habit she had kept since serving in the army. They had met overseas, during the Southeast China campaign, lost touch for almost twenty years, and met again in the New Babylonian police force. The labyrinths of life.

Ratner rubbed his chin. He was sitting at Jordan's desk, in her office. He got up and faced the captain, a massive tower of perfumed strength.

"Hmmm," he said. "Very unusual. Any theories?"

Jordan shook her head. "Not really, except for the usual political and social crap put forth by the usual bunch of self-proclaimed 'experts' in the media. But our people are actually baffled by this. I mean, there definitely are some similarities with the LSD and MDMA situations in the sixties and nineties, but even then, most of the dealers were small-time criminals working for bigger sharks. But here . . ."

"You mean you can't find a connection?"

"Exactly. They all got it from 'someone' who got it from 'someone,' etc. We managed to break a chain—or so we thought. See those four? One led to another. Last one on the line, same story. A law student, mind you. Closest we got to a criminal ring."

She let out a dry, lifeless laugh. Ratner suddenly felt like a cigarette, but he hadn't noticed an ashtray in Jordan's office.

"You think it's imported?"

The captain shrugged. "Who knows? That's what they say on TV. At least, what *some* say on TV."

This was a direct allusion to Rust. Apparently not her favorite.

"Yeah. I heard it too."

"Politics," she hissed. "More harmful than drugs."

Ratner nodded and smiled. He liked that last remark very much. "Indeed. So, what's your take? How do we deal with this? What would you need to become more effective?"

"More people, of course. But that won't happen, I know."

Ratner smiled apologetically. The last budget he had approved didn't look so good.

"The only way to get to the source is to infiltrate the network," Jordan resumed. "That's how it always works. But I've got a limited number of detectives, Georg. I need more workforce. Maybe you can speak in Tchebick's ear."

"Sure."

He was glad he didn't have to promise anything. He didn't want to be on bad terms with Jordan. She was a dedicated and a competent officer. Much more than he was, he thought.

"One last thing," he said, mimicking the famous Columbo line.

She got it and smiled. "Yes?"

"How dangerous is this drug, in your opinion?"

"Honestly, I don't know. First, it's fairly recent. Second, nobody really knows what secondary effects it has. Nobody's died of it and, so far, nobody has been committed to a psychiatric institution because of it. What's more, like LSD, it doesn't seem to be an addictive drug. Recreational use, as they say. But, if you look at it with our politicians' eyes, it can be seen as extremely dangerous—for the same reason LSD was. It's got nothing to do with health or crime issues, but it's about politics. Synth is a political drug, Georg. It makes people believe in other realities. It makes them escape the system. That's where the real danger is. That's what the system cannot tolerate."

Ratner nodded. "Thank you for your honesty, Eris. I'm glad to be working with you again."

They shook hands as he left. She had a surprisingly soft grip. Her perfume lingered around him for a while as he walked back to his car. It was a nice and comforting smell.

5

The bath was at the perfect temperature, and Ratner felt all the muscles in his body relax and melt like wax. He could hear Laura on the phone, pacing in the sitting room and laughing intermittently. His thoughts drifted to Captain Jordan. It was nice seeing her again, albeit in official circumstances. He hadn't seen her as a system critic, and her comments had pleased him. Maybe he should invite her to come for dinner one evening. He was sure she and Laura would find many common grounds and prepare the next revolution.

VI. THE LOVERS

The Lovers: A desire to grow things. Careless whispers. Wishing for summer. Two are two are one. The distance between things. Longing for a mountain trip.

1

Ratner walked into the interrogation room, followed by Captain Eris Jordan. He had asked her permission to interrogate one of the suspects in her Synth investigation. She had called him a couple days later and given him a time and a room number at the police station. Ratner had then informed Flowers, who told him he should talk to Commissioner Thomsen too, as the dealer had been arrested on his turf. Ratner had promised, but "forgotten" to comply. *Fuck Thomsen, fuck that little incompetent pretentious asshole*, he had thought. It seemed that wherever he went, he ran into that nasty idiot.

The suspect was a law student, twenty-four years old, described as Caucasian in the old racist terms, pale and nondescript in Ratner's own categories, looking both scared and dejected. The prison's dark blue suit contrasted violently with the general feeling of weakness projected by his demeanor, but matched nicely the dark circles under his eyes.

Ratner presented himself, but Jordan didn't. They had probably met before. The interrogation was courteous, the suspect obviously frightened and eager to cooperate. *Definitely not your usual hardened dealer type*, Ratner thought as he took notes of times and places. The kid explained that he got the batch of pills at a party organized by a fraternity on campus last July. He had asked around for some Synth and a girl had told him she had some. Ratner asked for a description. Tall, blonde, short hair, blue eyes, white tee, jeans, sneakers, foreign accent. She said her name was Vita. Good-looking, but not cute, he added, as if it helped. "We made a composite," Jordan whispered in Ratner's ear. "Doesn't help much. I'll show it to you later."

They had gone to the parking lot and she had given him a pill. The price was cheap and the kid thought about buying some for his friends and ended up getting a whole bag. She had given him a phone number to call in case he wanted more.

Ratner glanced at Jordan, sitting next to him.

"We checked it. Disposable phone. Disconnected."

The city commissioner nodded.

The kid had quickly sold his batch and made a good profit. So he called and met her again, in the parking lot of a cinema downtown. And a last time, one month ago, in another parking lot, behind another cinema. Her hair had grown, he noticed. But she still had an accent.

"What kind of accent?" Ratner asked.

"I don't know. German, maybe."

"We checked with the New Berlin embassy and the visa service," Jordan said. "But no real match. Or too many, if you will. I mean, blonde, blue eyes, and an accent—seriously? And of course, no girl named Vita on their lists."

"What about the composite?"

Captain Jordan turned on the tablet she had brought along and pressed and swiped a couple of times until a face appeared. The kid extended his neck to look at it too.

"Yeah, that's her," he said, although nobody had asked him.

Ratner looked at the image.

Jordan was right. Could be anybody.

Ratner's phone suddenly vibrated. A message. He took it out and looked at the screen. It was from Valentino. He wanted a place and a time to meet. Today. Ratner typed a time and Le Robespierre as a place. What the hell. At least he would get good music and a decent beer if the info was bad or useless. And he was sure he wouldn't run into Thomsen there.

2

Thinking of the devil, Ratner mused as they walked out of the interrogation room to find Commissioner Thomsen waiting for them outside. He was obviously fuming, although he couldn't vent his anger at Ratner, as the city commissioner was his superior. His tight face was flustered, the gray eyes icy behind the small rectangular glasses. You could feel him struggling not to explode. In a way, it was a funny sight. To Ratner at least.

"Captain Jordan, there is a strict chain of command in *my* department (he stressed the *my* so much Georg had to suppress a chuckle) that I would like you to observe. I should have been informed of this interrogation, and your attitude will be duly noted in the report I shall send to DA Flowers."

Thomsen turned around, diva-like, and left them in the long corridor. He walked fast, like a cartoon character, and let the door slam behind him.

"And hello to you too," Ratner mumbled, winking at Jordan. "Don't worry, Flowers is a close friend of mine. I'll take the blame."

The captain shook her head. "Ah, no worries. He's just a fucking asshole. Nobody likes him. He only got where he is because he's good at licking asses. Certainly not because of his competence."

Ratner nodded. Yes, he would definitely have to invite her over for dinner. They would all have plenty of things to discuss.

3

Ratner told his driver to make a detour by the city's old cemetery. He considered his day done and needed some time alone. The gray afternoon sky had broken into a light drizzle, covering everything with a shiny varnish. He thought of Barbara when she was doing her toenails in the summer. She used transparent gloss. Laura preferred dark colors, like crimson or navy blue, even black sometimes. He wondered if this said anything about a person's soul. If so, what color was his soul? What would he choose for his nails? He shifted his position on the backseat. Yellow. Of course. A bright, bright yellow. A warm, blinding and gaudy color.

4

He walked up to Barbara's grave, his feet slightly sliding on the wet gravel. There was no special reason for him to stop there today, and why should there be, after all? You never have to have a reason to see someone you love. Or loved. Which actually was the same thing when that person was dead. Or someone you missed. Or both, as in Barbara's case.

He stopped in front of the small marble headstone inscribed with her name and dates. A whole life reduced to letters and numbers. Good memories flowed over his body like comforting incense smoke. He missed her still, although he was happy to be with Laura. The eternal question, "is it possible to love two people equally?" had a simple answer: yes. Equally and differently, two different planes, superimposed but not joined. A complex geometrical figure, imposed by fate. Life was made purely of what we had, its materiality bound us, and it was the only thing we couldn't negate. But dreams, hopes and feelings were part of that materiality too.

Barbara was still here, transformed into something we prosaically called time and poetically memory. It always made him happy to come and visit her. It made him feel whole, at one with the strange world he was living in and rebuilding every day. He blew a silent kiss and began to walk back to the car. It had stopped raining. Everything shone beautifully.

5

Valentino was sitting at a small table in a corner of Le Robespierre, a fresh pint of lager in front of him. He was scribbling in a little notebook, a leather attaché case at his feet. Ratner waved at him while ordering his drink at the bar.

"This place is so you," Valentino said as the city commissioner sat down in front of him. "It feels like being inside your brain."

"I'll take it as a compliment," Ratner grumbled. "What was that you were writing down? Poetry?"

Valentino smiled and Ratner thought he saw him blush slightly in the bad electric light.

"Yes. Well, not exactly. Ideas for poems."

Ratner raised his glass. "To poetry, then."

They cheered.

"To change the subject and get back to prose: did you manage to find anything?"

Valentino nodded, putting the notebook in the inside pocket of his jacket. He lifted his attaché case and patted it.

Ratner noticed the captain's watch, which looked like a 1960s model. "Nice watch, by the way. Is it a real vintage one?"

"Yes, it was my father's. Thank you. Now, to go back to my case, it's only raw material still, but I think it's big. Like really, really big."

Ratner waited. He remembered Valentino. The guy could be enthusiastic about finding a half-smoked cigarette on a crime scene, only to learn afterward that a cop had carelessly dropped it earlier.

"Remember when you asked me why the guy had sent me this email? Well, your question bugged me and I decided to check my spam box. Guess what? He had sent me an email about three weeks before he got killed, asking me to contact him, then another one the day before he sent the last one, begging me to call him and giving me his number."

"Wow," Ratner said. "And both emails were in the spam box, but not the last one?"

"Yes. Crazy, isn't it? I feel bad now. I should have checked before."

Ratner shrugged. "I never check my spam box," he said, in a manner of consolation. "Not your fault."

Jesse nodded like a soldier accepting an order from his general. "So, anyway, I went to Green Star's offices with the warrant you signed and asked for access to Harding's workstation. Turns out he had a laptop, which was still in his office."

"Really?" Ratner interrupted. "How convenient."

"Exactly, right? So I thanked them and took it back downtown for our guys to check it out."

"And?"

"Nothing. Of course."

"Of course," Ratner repeated mechanically.

"The guys told me the computer had been reformatted."

"Figures."

"Yes, but they didn't do such a good job, apparently. Amateurs, according to our guys. They were able to recover some files." Valentino pointed at his attaché case. "I managed to print a lot of stuff, because I don't like to read on a screen. I also have it on a USB key, just to be safe." He patted the front of his jacket.

"What's the stuff you printed?"

"Spreadsheets mostly. Haven't had time to really check it out, of course, but it looks very promising." The captain raised his glass. "To justice," he said.

"I have a question," Ratner said, after wiping some foam off his upper lip.

"Shoot."

"Why did you want to see me? Here? I mean, I know I chose the place, but you didn't want to see me in your office. Or mine, for that matter."

Valentino leaned forward, almost whispering. "It's because I don't want any witness to our meeting. And also because our offices could be bugged. I know I sound paranoid, but trust me, this is big . . . I mean, it could become political."

What doesn't in this city? Ratner thought, but decided to keep his cynicism to himself. "I see," he said, meaning: *yes, you do sound completely paranoid.*

Ratner looked at his watch, trying to find an excuse to end the meeting, which was becoming a little bit too strange for his taste. "I'm sorry," he said, "But I promised Laura to be home early."

Ratner felt himself cringe inside. He absolutely hated using Laura as an excuse, especially since she was the most open and tolerant person he had ever met. Even Barbara could get annoyed with him and wouldn't hide her displeasure. But Laura . . . she was a saint in his eyes.

"I understand," Valentino said, picking up his attaché case. "I'm lucky to be living alone."

The city commissioner couldn't sense any trace of bitterness in the captain's words. Only Valentino could say something like that. Maybe the man meant it. Hell, he probably meant it. He was glad not to be stuck with him in a car for an eight-hour shift anymore.

6

Ratner was watching a documentary about Synth on his laptop when Laura walked into the apartment.

"I ordered some pizza," he said as she hung her coat in the corridor. "There is some left for you in the kitchen."

"Thank you," she said, "but I ate after the meeting. I had a sandwich with Mary and the other girls."

She moved into the sitting room, preceded by her smell—a discrete mixture of sweat, perfume and tobacco. *They should make a perfume out of it*, he thought. *Wonderfully intoxicating.*

"What are you watching?" she asked, bending over his right shoulder.

"Some documentaries about Synth," he said. "It's for work. Flowers wants me to crack down on the stuff. It's on Delgado's agenda. Rust is using it against her."

"He's using *everything* against her. He would use his own mother against her. Then again, she kind of deserves it too."

Ratner nodded despite himself. Although he didn't agree with all of Laura's revolutionary stance, she did have a couple of good points—and Delgado's presidency sure wasn't brilliant on many issues.

"I actually would like to try some," she said, getting herself a glass of wine in the kitchen. He heard the clinking of the glass and the liquid being poured.

"Really? You're serious?"

"What? Not you?"

Ratner looked at his glass of whisky sitting next to the laptop. "Hell, no! Why would I want to do that?"

Laura sat in front of him, on the other side of the table.

"Supposedly, you can create a whole universe and turn it on or off as you please. The ultimate escape."

Ratner nodded, a little uneasy. "Why would I want to escape?"

Laura looked at him, arching her eyebrows. "Are you serious? You like this life? This world?"

"Yes. Well, no, but still . . . it's real. You can't escape it. You've got to accept it and do something about it to make it better."

Laura took a long sip of her wine. "You really sound like a cop, sometimes."

"I am a cop."

She got up to sit on the couch and turn the TV on.

"I am a cop," he repeated, uncertain it was for her or for himself.

7

The ringing of his mobile phone woke him up like the buzzing of a huge mosquito. He felt like slapping it as he grabbed it. Then, hearing the news, he felt like destroying it even more.

"What's going on?" Laura asked, still half-asleep. "What time is it?"

"A colleague has been murdered. I have to go check it out."

"Ah shit," Laura mumbled. "Good luck, then."

She was already asleep when he slammed the door behind him.

VII. THE CHARIOT

The Chariot: Buying a new car. Thinking about the future. A contest of cities. Dressing up your dog as a sphinx. Remembering that black and white are not colors. Remembering everything and moving further.

1

"Ah, City Commissioner, this way, please."

Ratner followed the officer into the dead-end street, the large uniformed silhouette shimmering in the red and blue lights of the police vehicles. Ratner immediately recognized the body lying under the scrutiny of the paramedics.

As they stopped, the officer began, "His name is—"

"Jesse Valentino. I know him."

"Sorry to hear," the cop said, and Ratner nodded. Condolences between cops were always sincere.

He stepped forward, looking at the body. Valentino was lying on his back, eyes wide open. There was no apparent wound.

"Stabbed from behind," the officer said, as if he had read his mind. "Went right into the heart. Either a lucky shot or a professional. He was probably killed on the main street, then dragged here. His wallet was found next to the body. No money nor credit cards in it, of course. Only his badge."

Ratner rubbed his eyes. "Any idea of the time?"

The officer shook his head. "Two kids who wanted some crack found him. Best deterrent against drugs, a dead body. No offense meant, sorry. I forgot he was your friend."

Ratner shrugged. "Not a friend, really. We used to be partners, before he switched to the Finance Bureau. Long time ago."

"Well, sorry anyway. When they found him, he was cold. The blood had dried."

The city commissioner looked at his shoes. He was standing on a darker hue of asphalt. Dried blood. He side-stepped and asked for a pair of latex gloves.

He motioned to the two paramedics to move aside and crouched next to the body. He went through his pockets, purposely avoiding looking at his dead friend's face.

"We already gathered his stuff," the officer said. He called out to a female officer, who came over holding a small plastic bag.

"We also found a discarded kebab sandwich on the main street sidewalk," the woman said. "Could explain what he was doing here."

Ratner nodded and looked at the two objects in the bag. A wallet. A USB stick. No watch. No keys. "That's it? No keys? Did you send someone to check his apartment?" Ratner, asked, alarmed.

"Well . . . no," the officer said. "Didn't think of it."

"Shit," Ratner said. He began running toward his car.

2

Valentino's apartment looked like a hurricane had run through it.

"Damn," Ratner said, looking at the disaster.

The keys were still in the door, which was left half-open. Ratner's assigned driver, a young Asian officer with a tight muscular frame, stepped in behind him. "Wow," he said.

"Call for backup," Ratner said. "Although it's too late."

3

Ratner shut the report on Valentino's murder and massaged his eyelids. It was a copy Commissioner Millborne, who was in charge of the district where Valentino's body had been discovered, had discreetly sent him.

It had been three days now since the murder, and Ratner was becoming impatient. Some things didn't add up in the general picture. The captain had been murdered, possibly in a mugging attempt, although the wound had been extremely precise—the blade had gone right through the heart, from behind. *Professional,* his inner detective voice nagged him. *Professional!* But he refused to listen to it. Yet. Only the money and the credit cards had been lifted from Valentino's wallet, plus his keys.

His apartment had been searched and his computer was gone, as well as his attaché case. *Professional! Professional!* But the murderer had forgotten the USB key in the captain's pocket, which was now being analyzed by the guys of the Technical Section—he knew Lieutenant Marvin Bailey there, who would forward him their findings.

Although Flowers had told him to assign all the available men to the case, Ratner knew that only a couple were maybe available, and he also felt it was his responsibility to crack this one. And something else was nagging him, although he couldn't put his finger on it.

He stood up, buzzed Mrs. Gardiner for a coffee—black, no sugar—and walked to the huge window. New Babylon lay there as it always did, in this dull gray late fall morning. Another name had been added to the list of its victims, this time one of a friend. He frowned as he looked down on the traffic and the tiny changing lights. Could he call Valentino a friend? They had been partners, sure. But they hadn't seen each other in years until the captain had walked in with his suspicions about Green Star, or whatever that company was called.

He looked through the file again to find the list of items recovered on the body. He read it twice before it struck him. There was no notebook mentioned.

Of course, this could have meant nothing. Valentino might have kept the notebook at home, on a table or in a drawer somewhere. But Ratner felt he had to make sure. He took out his phone and called Sergeant Chambers, his assigned driver. The officer could file for overtime now. If Ratner carried on like this, he would be rich soon.

4

"No, nothing, City Commissioner."

Ratner nodded at Officer Chambers, standing in the bedroom's doorway. He hadn't found the notebook anywhere either. Valentino's apartment still looked like Dresden in 1944. He shut the light as they left and bowed under the yellow ribbon barring the door. *Death is an untidy bastard*, he thought, as they waited for the elevator.

5

When Ratner finally got home, it was half past seven and Laura wasn't there. Taking off his leather coat, he remembered she had vaguely told him about some meeting. He was late because he'd had to go back to his office to take care of some administrative stuff, and Flowers had called him to talk about the Synth issue. Ratner told him about Valentino, and that he was interested in investigating the case.

"Sure," Flowers had said. "I would do the same. Hope you nail the bastard. Let me know if I can be of any help. But Synth is a priority right now. You've got to focus on the problem and find me some of their dealers, laboratories, whatever. It's on top of your list, Georg, and it has to stay there. Promise? Sorry about your friend again."

Politics, politics and more politics. But at least Ratner felt that his ass was covered for now, although it was only in a phone conversation. It was never seen well when superiors took over cases—political suspicions immediately arose.

Sighing, he turned on the TV. As if on cue, there was an interview with Todd Bailer, a specialist of psychedelics and weird science who had his own show on cable TV.

"What are the known effects of Synth?" the journalist, a young black woman with short hair, was asking him.

Bailer, a middle-aged man with a good face and gray fuzzy hair, answered her as best he could, given "he hadn't personally tried it."

Ratner had met Bailer a couple of times at dinners and parties organized by their common friend, Sheryl Boncoeur, the NBTV host. Although Bailer resided in New Petersburg, Ratner would give him a call and hear his personal opinion about the drug and its origins.

The documentary went on about how Synth affected New Babylon and its subcultures. They mentioned music. Ratner poured himself a tall glass of whisky and sat down with interest. He loved music and was open to any new sound, even if influenced by devil-inspired drugs. *The best kind, actually*, he thought, with an ironic smirk.

"Like in the sixties, where LSD became a reference to music, and in the nineties with Ecstasy and the Manchester scene, Synth is setting down its mark with a new genre called DAO—in capitals. Darren Deich is the founder of Synth Records. Darren, what is DAO?"

The young man looked like a 1950s conservative, with slick hair parted on the side, a white shirt, a thin black tie and a set of classical Colonel Sanders-style glasses. The only things that contradicted his McCarthy commission–supporter look were the three earrings on his left ear and the piercing on his right eyebrow.

"DAO cannot be described," he answered. "That's why it's called DAO."

He then refused to give a further explanation. Ratner wrote down the name of the guy and his record company. He might pay him a visit one of these days. They could discuss music, maybe.

6

Ratner hadn't heard Laura come in, and he was startled when she put her hand on his shoulder. He was still sitting at the table, in front of his laptop with his large expensive Bluetooth earphones—a recent birthday present—over his ears.

"What are you doing?" Laura asked.

"Listening to some Synth music," he answered, as if it was obvious.

"You mean, stuff like Tangerine Dream or Klaus Schulze?" she said, surprised. "I thought you hated that Kraut stuff."

"I love Kraut rock," Georg précised. "Like Can or Guru-Guru. But, yes, I hate German seventies synthesizer music. And no, that's not what I'm talking about. I'm listening to music inspired by the drug called Synth."

"Really?"

"Yes. It's part of my job."

Laura eyed the bottle of whisky and the glass with the half-melted ice cube floating in pale yellow liquid. "Drinking alone? Not fair."

She went into the kitchen and came back with a glass containing a few ice cubes. She poured herself a good dose and sat down next to him. "Any good?" she said.

"I actually like it a lot."

Ratner turned off his earphones and the music flowed through the computer's tinny built-in speakers. It was complicated and fascinating, with entwined melodies and a slow bass line, like water flowing over water, in different currents and hues. There was an underlying tension, too, which made the whole thing highly enjoyable and somewhat mind-boggling.

"Not bad," Laura said. "Who is it?"

Ratner peered at the player on his screen. "Wagon Seven."

"Never heard of them," Laura said.

"Me neither," he said. "Just discovered them through a documentary on Synth. And where were you?"

"Oh, at a union meeting, again. We might strike. The union is seriously considering it, and I agree."

Ratner grunted. "What's the problem? Why do you want to strike?"

Laura looked at him with arched eyebrows. Even when making faces, he found her beautiful. "Are you kidding me?"

He timidly shook his head.

"Haven't you watched the news? Paid attention to what I have been telling you almost every night? The government cuts are hitting us really hard. You know the kind of kids I'm working with, right? In my class, we have two twelve-year-olds who need three strong men to accompany them everywhere, because they are so violent. Well, we've just learned that they're going to let some of the helpers go. We can't function without these people, Georg. These kids can't do anything by themselves."

Ratner vaguely remembered the complaints he had heard about overtime in his own department. He had blamed them on the new generation who couldn't handle a little stress, as they could in the old days. Maybe he should listen more before things got really ugly. Or, then again, maybe they were just wimps.

"So we're going to vote about a strike next week."

Ratner poured some whisky over his dying ice cube in a gesture of mercy. "Is that the only way?" he asked. "Delgado said it was necessary to do those cuts. Because of the economic crisis. You're not alone in this. We suffer, too, in the police department."

When Tchebick learned that the wife of his city commissioner was organizing a strike in her school, he would go ballistic.

"Exactly. Your guys should strike too."

Hadn't she been the one mentioning walls falling down, when he got promoted? How about the roof falling down too?

Laura downed her glass and said she was going to bed.

"I'll join you in a minute," he said.

He put his earphones back on and played some more of that DAO. Tonight he almost felt like trying Synth.

VIII. FORTITUDE

Fortitude: Meeting a goddess in a dream. A desire for fresh air. Buying a new pet. Thinking about Switzerland. Something invisible holding everything into place. Violence morphing into game.

1

This morning was going to be a phone call morning. Ratner moved a pile of files from his desk, making some room for a steaming mug of coffee. He looked for his address book in the inner pocket of his jacket and threw it next to the mug. He then picked up a pen and rummaged in his desk drawer to find a blank sheet of paper, which proved more difficult than he had expected.

The morning sky hung like a dull shower curtain outside the large windows of his office. November was slowly dying, and December was closing in, all dressed up in various layers of blacks and grays. Some would find it depressing, but Ratner disagreed. Winter was just another kind of specific ugliness which, when added to this city, made her beautiful in a new, melancholic and inspiring way.

2

"Allô?"

"Todd? This is Georg. Georg Ratner, from New Babylon."

"Ah, Georg! Good to hear from you! What's up?"

"What's the time in Petersburg? I'm not waking you up, I hope."

"No, no."

Todd Bailer, the border-science show-host laughed his good warm laugh on the other end. "We're three hours behind. It's seven thirty right now. I'm drinking my coffee."

"I can never keep it straight, with all these summer and winter times. Can't remember if it's a three- or four-hours difference."

"Well, it's three. Most of the time."

They laughed.

"Listen," Ratner resumed, "I just saw you on television, in a documentary on Synth. I don't know how bad the problem is in Petersburg, but here, it's getting out of hand and the authorities are becoming worried." *I sound like a fucking politician.* Ratner cringed, alone in his office.

"So I wanted to hear your expert opinion," he continued, "both on the drug and the phenomenon. Any idea where Synth comes from? I can't find any decent info on it."

"I know, that's what's mind-boggling to me too," Bailer said. "I wanted to do a show on the stuff, and it was axed. Seems that there's a lot going on around this drug. I'm not even sure we're not being monitored right now."

"Are you serious?"

Bailer made a strange sound, between a sigh and a grunt. "Actually, yes. Not too sure if it's safe to talk about it on the phone, or by email. But we're meeting soon, right?"

Ratner was surprised. He hadn't made any plans to go to New Petersburg, at least while he was sober. "How do you mean?"

"Sheryl hasn't contacted you? I actually thought that this was the reason you called."

"No, she hasn't. What's the deal?"

"She wants to invite us—just us—to discuss Synth on her show."

Ratner's brains warped to hyperspeed. Sheryl was close to President Delgado. This was obviously a political stunt.

"I see. When?"

"Next week. Wednesday, I think. She said she would email me the details today."

"Okay. Perfect, then. Let me know when you arrive. We could maybe meet before or after the show."

"Yes. Let's."

Ratner threw the silent phone on the top of his desk. He needed a cigarette. He needed some poison that cleared the mind, not blurred it.

3

His private cell phone rang just at the moment he crushed his cigarette. He recognized Sheryl Boncoeur's number and accepted the call, waving the smoke away.

"Georg?"

"Synchronicity," Ratner answered. "I was talking to Todd Bailer ten minutes ago."

"Oh, you were? Excellent! Did he tell you about the show next week?"

Sheryl's show, *Holding No Punches*, was a famous news-centered talk show airing every Wednesday on NBTV. It was famous because it was live and, as its name subtly indicated, Sheryl really held no punches with her guests. To be invited was both an honor and a curse.

"He actually did. And yes, thank you for your invitation, if that is why you called."

"Indeed it was. So glad you can come. It will be a great show."

"Just one question, though: why Synth? I mean why now?"

"Well, as you probably know better than me, Synth has become an issue recently, so I thought relevant to bring it up."

"You mean, since Rust has been using it in his campaign against Delgado?"

Sheryl laughed her beautifully smooth laughter. "Ah, Georg, always the detective looking for suspects. You know what the audience wants."

"Blood?"

"Yes, and bread. You and Bailer will be the bread, of course. I'm not doing this for a kill, if you want to know. On the contrary. I will be glad to support you on this, if you know what I mean."

"I think I do, indeed. Thank you in any case. I'll be glad to appear on your show."

Sheryl laughed again and hung up. *That woman*, Ratner thought, *was a million times more dangerous than Synth.* But he had to admit he appreciated her, and very much so. As a journalist, she was ruthless, but she did actually have a self-appointed mission: to expose all of the city's hypocrisies and lies. She was the mirror that New Babylon both loved and feared. And sometimes he liked to imagine that of himself too.

4

Ratner looked at his list of upcoming calls and wondered if he should wait or go ahead with the next one. It was the call he feared the most, the one he knew was going to fuck things up and put him in a mess. He knew this, not because he was a psychic, but because of the sad reality, Laura had reminded him, of the state of things in the public services of the city.

New Babylon was a mess.

Pure and simple.

Some people said that something good can come out of chaos, but Ratner knew better: only chaos comes out of chaos. And never for the better.

Although he disliked Rust with all that was left of his humanist heart, he had to admit that his attacks on President Delgado did have a ground. All the cuts her government had made because of the recent financial crash—caused by candidate Rust's best friends, which was doubly ironic—had made her very unpopular among her usual supporters: the remnants of the working class, intellectuals and the liberal middle classes.

Laura was the perfect example of this. Or rather, her anger was. And Ratner knew it was justified, although he couldn't see how Delgado could have managed otherwise, unless she had jailed all the corrupt bankers and seized their money and assets, as a medieval queen would have done. Unfortunately, the times weren't that simple anymore, or maybe just complicated in other ways, as Delgado's last campaign had been supported by "rich anonymous donors," who everybody knew were precisely the aforementioned bankers—who were also officially supporting her opponent at the time. Money doesn't care about politics, they say. Ratner saw this as a very sad truth that every politician should be reminded of on the very evening of their election.

5

The call to Northern District Commissioner Thomsen had been short, but to the point. He had no detective to spare on Valentino's murder, or rather, there were two detectives on the case, but given the recent budget cuts, they already had to work overtime, and: "even though Valentino was one of us, he was obviously murdered by some junkie, and we all know how that goes, right, very sorry, but if they find anything, you will be the first one to know, of course. Thank you for calling, City Commissioner. Goodbye."

Ratner angrily buzzed in Mrs. Gardiner and asked her for a strong coffee.

His thoughts drifted to Jesse Valentino, as he watched the whirls of smoke escape the Styrofoam cup. The poet-cop. The *unknown* poet-cop. His lips stretched in a bittersweet smile and he typed "Jesse Valentino" in the search engine.

To his complete surprise, the man seemed to have quite a following—numerous literary blogs around the world mentioned his name or had reviewed his collection, which had more than 253 entries on the most popular online readers' site, with an average star-rating of 4.73 out of 5. "Unknown at home, famous everywhere else," the city commissioner whispered, scrolling down the screen. *That would make a good epitaph*, he chuckled somberly.

He tried to order Valentino's latest collection, as a belated tribute, but the book wasn't available online.

"Typical," Ratner grunted. He decided to go to a bookstore later. That would be a good break from the boring and predictable routine visits linked to his new job.

6

"Sorry, sir, but we don't carry any poetry collections—apart from the classics, because they're on the university's syllabus, of course—but they don't sell, you see, and we're a business. You know what I mean, and yes, it is sad, I personally *love* poetry, but we're part of a big chain, you know, so we can't decide what products we sell, bestsellers mostly, I mean, only, ah ah ah, the rest you can easily get on the internet, so I mean, it's not completely tragic, and no, I can't think of a bookseller that would have it, not in New Babylon anyway, maybe you should try the publisher, they usually know where you can get their books, have a nice day, hope to see you soon, and did you have any other author in mind, perhaps? Someone famous, maybe?"

7

Leaving the bookstore Ratner couldn't help comparing in his mind the raving reviews of Valentino's poetry and the impossibility of buying it in a bookstore.

Then again, maybe that was what made it so special: untainted by the mainstream shit-monster. He thought about all those weird jazz albums he himself loved, and that documentary he had watched on DAO music. The interesting things were never directly commercial. Even as a cop he could see that the underground was a treasure trove for culture.

"Duuuh!" Laura would have said. And she would have been right. A few drops of rain fell on his shoulders, like heavy fingers trying to make their point. He hurried toward the subway station. No need to be depressed *and* soaking wet.

IX. THE HERMIT

The Hermit: Power shortage. A desire to wear your mother's nightgown. Winter solstice. To be alone and happy. To reflect upon the discovery of electricity. Waiting for someone to appear you can beat up with your cane. Trying to grow a beard. Wisdom of the seasons.

1

Ratner closed the last file and sighed. He took a cigarette out of its package and lit it, inhaling deeply. He had spent the last two days reviewing all the info and police reports on Synth trafficking, but it seemed that all leads were coming to a dead-end.

Opium, heroin and morphine came from the Chinese Confederation, cocaine and weed came from the Bolivarian Republic, amphetamine and most designer drugs were locally produced, but nobody had a clue on Synth. It was if the drug had magically appeared out of nowhere. Unknown a year ago, and now a prime-time talk-show topic.

One theory suggested terrorists in New Petersburg. Another version claimed it was a secret weapon designed by New Moscow. The most credible rumor referred to a military drug developed in Viborg City. The only problem was that Viborg City was a staunch ally of the Western Alliance, led by New Babylon, and that it categorically denied having anything to do with it.

True or untrue, it was a delicate diplomatic situation and Ratner knew he couldn't go there. He would make a few phone calls, to be legit, but wouldn't push anything unless they themselves offered to collaborate.

His thoughts drifted to that guy he had seen in the interview on Synth-inspired music, Warren Deich. He looked like a straight-edge kind of guy, but it was hard to imagine a puritan producing drug-fueled music. It would be like a hippie rock 'n' roll producer who didn't smoke weed. Deich had to have connections. He had to. Ratner scribbled down his name on a piece of paper and underlined it three times.

2

New Babylon was half-eaten by the fog, the skyscrapers looking like lone concrete, steel and glass islands isolated on a frozen sea. It reminded him of a painting of an icy mountain landscape by the German Romantic artist Caspar David Friedrich, which hung in the New Babylonian Museum of Art. Ratner brought the warm coffee mug to his lips, its steam adding a blur to the landscape. Although his office was well heated, he felt chilly inside. Maybe he should find the time to go and see this painting again. Art always warmed his soul.

3

In the cafeteria Ratner ran into Jim Flowers carrying a tray with various small vegan delicacies and a cup of cinnamon-smelling Chai.

"Mind if I join you?" the city commissioner asked.

"Not at all," the DA answered. "I'll be over there."

A few minutes later Ratner sat in front of Flowers, a thick roast-beef sandwich on his own tray, and a beer.

"All the same, all different," Flowers joked, eyeing Ratner's lunch.

"Fortunately," Ratner answered. "What a boring world it would be otherwise. I mean, even more boring."

"So, how are things, Georg?"

Sitting in a public place, surrounded by colleagues that had well-trained ears and eyes, Ratner knew he had to be careful.

"Could be better, could be worse," he said. "Depends on how you want to look at it."

"I see," Flowers said, nodding. "Any progress, though?"

Ratner shrugged. "There will be. There has to be, if I understood you correctly."

Flowers nodded again. "And what about your colleague? The one who was murdered?"

"Nothing yet. I'm waiting for the officers in charge to call me, but they are already overworked I've been told."

"Like all of us, " Flowers sighed.

Ratner didn't answer. He had never seen himself as overworked. He did what he had to do, and if it was a lot, then it was a lot. It was simply the way he was, just as he was a faithful man in his relationships. Nothing to brag about and definitely not an example to others: people were free to do whatever they wanted, as far as he was concerned, as long as they didn't hurt anyone and mostly abided by the law.

4

Laura was home when he walked in, talking on the phone with someone he couldn't identify—a colleague, maybe.

After pouring himself a whisky, he sat down on the couch and turned the news channel on. Laura had disappeared into the bedroom. He could hear her muffled voice through the door.

Ted Rust's face appeared, perfect and beautiful as always. Compared to Maggie Delgado's tired and wrinkled face, he sure looked appetizing. The woman was barely sixty-one but she looked seventy—and that was on a good day. Of course, her term had been a rough one, starting with the end of the worst economic crisis the city ever experienced, and the never-ending flow of refugees from the various countries the Western Alliance military was involved in.

Rust was giving a speech in front of a full stadium, regularly interrupted by cheers and applause. He held his audience in his grip and was clearly enjoying it. The way he projected his jaw forward made Ratner think of a handsome Mussolini, although he wasn't fond of historical comparisons. Rust was his own, a filthy rich and powerful businessman turned politician by circumstances, with a xenophobic and ultra-capitalist agenda.

The fact that he was very corrupt could actually be seen a positive aspect in the city commissioner's eyes: his greed ironically made him human somehow—he wasn't invincible, he wasn't godlike, he had to wipe his ass like everybody else.

Compared to him, Maggie Delgado and her "let's work it out together" stance sounded dull and artificial. She looked like a banker, and talked like one, although she pretended her heart was on the left, red and bleeding.

But fewer and fewer voters bought this, according to the latest polls. They saw a tin-can heart painted red, which actually was a camouflaged moneybox. Hell, that's how he saw her too. But now he was indirectly working for her, because of Flowers and Tchebick, and although it was anything but glamorous, he also felt it was better to defend incompetence than to promote tyranny.

Laura fell on the couch next to him.

"The bastard is going to win," she sighed.

"Sure hope not," he grunted and took a sip of his whisky.

Laura held her hand out in front of him.

"I need some poison too," she said.

He watched her gulp the rest of the drink from the corner of his eye and found her beautiful. She put the glass down and wiped her lips with the back of her hand.

Leaning over him, she reached for her handbag, which lay crumpled beside him.

Rust had disappeared, replaced by political commentators trying to make sense of his speech. Laura rolled a thin joint and lit it up. The strong smell of weed floated under the city commissioner's nose.

"When Rust comes to power, this will probably be illegal again," he said, " and I will have to arrest you."

He picked up the joint from Laura's fingers and took a long hit.

"I have filmed everything, " she answered, "and will put it out on YouTube if you threaten me. Look over there, I planted a small camera above our TV set. You are so busted, Commissioner!"

"I will tell them you made me do it, you anarchist devil."

"Nobody will ever suspect such a pure and perfect lady, darling. I am but an innocent teacher!"

They kissed, lightly at first, then she took his head between her hands and held him while she inserted her soft warm tongue between his eager lips. He slipped a hand under her shirt, and she lifted her thigh against his hip.

The joint kept burning for a little while in the ashtray, then quietly died. No one picked it up.

5

Ratner rolled on his side to look at Laura, lying naked on her back next to him. Her soft breasts were heaving as she slowly caught her breath.

"Wow," she said. "Just wow."

They had moved to their bed to make love. The room was dark, lit only by the corridor's light bulb, which they had left on.

"Yeah," Ratner said, "I heard Rust has this effect on women."

Laura slapped his shoulder softly.

"Eeew," she grimaced.

They both laughed, sighed and Laura cuddled up against him. Holding her in his arms Ratner wondered if love was really as strong as some believed it was, or just incredibly stronger.

6

Ratner had just sent Mrs. Gardiner to fetch him a cup of coffee when Todd Bailer called him.

"Hey big guy! I'm in town. We talked about seeing each other before the show tonight. Still up for it?"

"Sure. Where do you want to meet?"

"No idea. I don't live here."

Ratner gave him the address of Le Robespierre.

"We can eat there too."

"Excellent," Bailer said. "Looking forward to seeing you again!"

"Same here. At six, Le Robespierre."

"*Oui, oui!*"

Ratner looked at December painting the morning with all sorts of chilly grays. It would be good to warm up with a great guy around a fresh beer. Or two.

7

A thought struck the city commissioner at the moment Mrs. Gardiner walked in, holding his cup of joe. He had not been contacted by Valentino's superior once since the captain's death. Hell, he didn't even know who his superior was. He searched quickly on the intranet, found the name—Commissioner Dany Lacroix—and picked up his phone.

"Commissioner Lacroix? City Commissioner Ratner."

There was a short silence at the other end of the line.

"Yes, sir?"

"I was checking on the case of Captain Valentino, who was murdered last week."

"Yes?"

"Do you happen to have any information that could be useful on the matter?"

Another silence.

"No ... I don't think so, at least. I'm not in charge of the investigation, you know."

"Yes, I know. I just thought you might have information that could be meaningful in the case."

"Well, no, I can't think of anything."

"Did Valentino ever mention a company named Green Star? He told me he was onto something about them."

A long sigh. "Did they contact you? I told Valentino to drop the case."

"Why did you tell him that?"

Another sigh. "Maybe we should discuss this in my office, Commissioner."

"Sure. I can be there at two. Would that be okay with you?"

"Fine."

The plot thickens, Ratner thought as he put the phone down. The question was: what plot?

8

Captain Lacroix was a jovial bald black man, athletically built with piercing black eyes, and a strong handshake. Ratner realized it was the first time he had walked into an office of the Finance Division. It looked like a bank office, clean, neat, impersonal. The only human touch was a picture of Lacroix's wife and their little boy on the desk.

"I know, it's very austere," Lacroix said as Ratner sat down in front of him. "It goes with the job. We have to look serious and dedicated. Only one personal object allowed."

Ratner nodded and looked around him, absentmindedly. "Are you?" he asked, his eyes focusing on Lacroix again.

"Sorry?" Lacroix said, confused.

"Serious and dedicated?"

The Finance Division Commissioner laughed heartily. "Yes, yes! Of course."

"Was Valentino?"

Lacroix immediately became serious again and rubbed his chin a couple of times. He had a stubble which reinforced his hard looks. "Let me put it this way: he was *very* serious and dedicated. Can I ask you a personal question, Commissioner?"

"Sure."

"How come you're so interested in Captain Valentino's murder? Nobody seems to care—it is about to be filed under "unsolved homicide," or something like that. I was told a junkie probably did him in. Is this personal? Did you know the captain?"

Ratner nodded. "Yes. We used to be partners, eons ago. I feel like I owe it to him."

Lacroix rubbed his chin another time, sat back in his chair, sighed, then leaned forward again, this time closer to Ratner. "Can we trust each other?"

Ratner shrugged. "I don't know. Can we?"

Lacroix smiled. "I would like to."

Ratner smiled back. He liked the guy. "Me too. Tell me what you know, and what you're not supposed to tell me," the city commissioner said.

"No, please tell me what you know first—so I build up from there."

Makes sense, Ratner thought approvingly. He briefly shared with Lacroix what Valentino had told him, and his suspicions about the company called Green Star.

"I see," Lacroix said. "He went to see you against my express orders. The guy was as stubborn as a mule."

And apparently a good poet too, Ratner thought, *even though that doesn't have anything to do with anything.* "Against your orders?"

"Yes—although they weren't exactly *my* orders, if you get my drift."

So here we are—the confidence test, Ratner mused. "Go ahead," Ratner said. "I guess Commissioner Thomsen is the one who pressured you."

Lacroix hesitated. "No, not directly anyway. It was weirder and more powerful than that. I got a direct phone call from Helena Gonzalez.The lawyer, you know?"

Ratner pursed his lips, regretting having shown his cards too early. On the other hand, if they were really doing the trust game, then it was okay that Thomsen's name was in the open.

"Yeah, I heard she is Green Star's legal representative. Big name for such a little company. I want to hear the whole story."

Lacroix nodded. "I guess we can trust each other now."

"I guess so too," Ratner agreed, smiling.

Lacroix extended a hand, which Ratner shook. They both had a strong grip and their knuckles turned slightly white.

"Okay . . . so Valentino came to see me with a story about this company and the whistle-blower who had contacted him and who had been found dead—same thing he told you. He asked me for a search warrant, but I told him that the evidence was too circumstantial. I had read that the guy's death had been filed as a suicide—even if I admit it stank a little."

Ratner smiled. "But he insisted . . ."

Lacroix nodded vigorously. "You know the guy. Yes, he insisted so much so that I told him I would ask my direct superior about it."

"Northern District Commissioner Thomsen—"

Lacroix nodded. The cat was out the bag for good now.

"—who told you there wasn't enough to go after and rejected the warrant? And that's when Gonzalez called you."

"Exactly. Wow, you should be a cop."

Ratner smiled. "Circumstantial evidence, eh?"

Lacroix shook his head and frowned. "And then Valentino goes rogue on me by asking you to sign the warrant and gets killed. I feel a level of responsibility in his death, I do admit."

Ratner shrugged. "Maybe Valentino *was* killed by a junkie, we don't know yet. Maybe there is nothing to sniff around Green Star. And although his wallet was stolen, he still had a USB key in the waist pocket of his jacket. It was very small—maybe the murderer didn't see it, or didn't care, because junkies only take what they can sell immediately. It's still at the tech lab, getting analyzed. I think so, at least. I will give them a call later. I'll let you know if there's anything interesting on it, or if we need your help with some of the data."

"Yes, please, do. I would really appreciate that."

They shook hands again, this time like friends. Ratner felt good as he walked out of the building. He had backup now. He wasn't completely on his own anymore. Of course, what were two idiots in the face of Thomsen's huge influence network? Well, two idiots, precisely. But if one idiot was harmless, two could be very dangerous.

9

"Sergeant Marvin Bailey, New Babylon Metropolitan Police Technical Department, what can I do for you?"

"Hi, Marvin. It's Georg. Checking on the USB key I sent you last week."

"Synchronicity. We finally managed to decrypt it."

"It was encrypted?"

Ratner had a hard time imagining Valentino knowing how to do this stuff. Then again, he hadn't realized his ex-colleague was an internationally recognized poet either.

"Yes. It's a free encryption program you can download from the web, but it's very, very efficient. Our computers have been working on it nonstop the past ten days. I'm sending you the zip file at this very moment. Looks like it's only spreadsheets. Tons of them. Enjoy."

Ratner thanked the sergeant and hung up. He walked toward the service car waiting to take him back to his office. One more piece added to the puzzle. If there was a puzzle, of course.

10

Todd Bailer was already sitting in front of a huge grilled cheese and jalapeños sandwich when Ratner stormed into Le Robespierre. Waving at his friend, the city commissioner walked to the bar to order a roast-beef sandwich and a beer.

"Sorry, I'm late," he apologized, sitting down, "but last minute things to take care of at the office."

Bailer smiled his benevolent smile and shook his head, which was covered with a jungle of frizzy gray hair. If one hadn't seen his show, he could have been easily mistaken for an aging hippie, minus the beard.

"No problem! Good to see you, Georg! This is a great place here. Love the music."

"Did you have a good trip?"

"Yes I did, thank you. I arrived early and did some shopping for the missus." He lifted a fancy paper bag with a golden brand name. "And you? What's up? Congratulations on your promotion, by the way. Sheryl told me. Must be a lot of work and responsibilities."

"Well, yes," Ratner grunted. "Especially with the elections coming up. That's actually why Sheryl invited us on her show. As you probably figured out."

"That Rust is scary," Bailer said, grabbing his beer. "Do you think he can win?"

Ratner nodded. "Oh yes. Very dangerous. Very clever. Huge media network and support. Not to mention his corporate friends. Honestly, I don't see how Delgado can stop him."

"Well, she still has a lot of support, no? People are angry at the economy, not at her, right? I mean, she tackled the crisis as best as she could, given the circumstances."

Ratner thought about Laura and shrugged. "Many of her supporters are unhappy. They think she did too much for her banker friends and not enough for the people. The cuts in the public services are very unpopular. There could be strikes soon."

Bailer put his glass down and wiped his lips. "Sounds like you were appointed at the worst of times."

Ratner nodded. He hadn't thought of his promotion exactly in those terms, but Bailer had a point. The question was: had he been appointed to save the day, or to become the sacrificial victim?

"So," Ratner said, wanting to change the subject. "What can you tell me about Synth that I should know but don't?"

Bailer sighed. "Like I told you on the phone the other day, it seems to be quite a politically sensitive topic. We also have this Synth counter-culture in New Petersburg now, which seems to be growing every day. Young people are really into it, and the authorities are terrified.

"Strangely enough, it doesn't seem to be an addictive drug, but an extremely recreational one. People don't get crazy, on the contrary, they are more sociable and open. There are even Synth communities now in Pete. Of course, they're treated like religious cults and everything, but I'm not sure they are. Not sure at all."

"Have you tried it?"

Bailer shook his head. "No, not yet," he laughed. "But I want to. I was planning to, for my show. Then it got canceled, as I told you on the phone."

"Yes. Very strange."

"Very indeed. I almost got scared, let me tell you. Sounded like I was becoming a national security threat and all."

They laughed.

"Well, it is definitely considered a security threat here," Ratner said. "Rust is using it against Delgado. Says we're not doing enough to fight the threat—whatever it is. I think Delgado's entourage pressured Sheryl to invite us. It will be a political show."

"Oh my God," Bailer winced. "What has she gotten me into? I hate politics."

"Don't worry, it won't be about you—but all about me. I'm the target here."

"You're lucky. I'm a terrible shooter."

"It's Sheryl I'm worried about. She's an excellent sniper."

Bailer chewed the last bit of his sandwich and sucked on his fingers. "True, but if she supports Delgado, she can't put you in a bad place. That would be stupid."

Ratner shrugged, pushing his sandwich on the plate. It was delicious, but he wasn't hungry. "We both know Sheryl. If she can smell blood, she will go into a frenzy, no matter what."

"Piranha Sheryl," Bailer offered.

"Exactly."

They raised their glasses.

"And you?" Bailer asked as they put down their pints. "Have you tried it?"

"What? Synth? Are you crazy?"

"No, seriously. Aren't you intrigued?"

"I'm a cop, Todd!" Ratner realized he had raised his voice a little and glanced around nervously. Nobody in the café knew about his job, or at least that's what he liked to imagine.

As no one seemed to have noticed, he continued in a lower tone, "I'm a cop and Synth is illegal. Period,"

Bailer smiled and tapped his friend's shoulder. "Come on, Georg. I was kidding. I won't ask you that during the show tonight, promise!"

"Good," Ratner said, raising the half-empty pint to his lips. "Good."

He couldn't help feeling a cold sweat break as the beer made its way down his throat.

11

"Georg! Todd! What a pleasure to see you both! So glad you accepted my invitation!"

Sheryl Boncoeur had stepped into the makeup room, smelling like a dream and looking like a very sexy Mrs. Robinson in a tight black dress.

Ratner waved as an assistant applied some thick face powder.

"Georg, I want you to know that Mayor Tchebick and DA Jim Flowers will be in the audience. Jim told me you had to see this as support and not control."

Ratner nodded. He knew it was *only* about control, and not at all about support. He smiled grimly.

"Please don't smile," the assistant said. "You're ruining my work."

12

In the cab taking him home from NBTV studios, Ratner felt surprisingly good. The show had gone well, and he felt he had given either satisfying answers or dodged Sheryl's bullets with extreme professionalism. Flowers had text-messaged him an emoji representing a "thumbs up." Support, not control, my ass.

Smiling, he reclined in the leather backseat. The cab driver was listening to some Ethiopian jazz. "Mulatu Astatke?" Ratner asked.

"No, Getachew Mekuria. You know?"

"Yes, a little bit. Wonderful music."

The driver nodded, his Afro swinging in the darkness of the cabin, and then proceeded to give the city commissioner a complete crash course on Ethiopian jazz and its roots. Ratner listened, jotting down a few names, and checking their spelling. This was one of the many reasons he loved this city so much: you never knew what your next lesson was going to be about.

13

Laura was still up when he walked in, watching TV. The routine of long-time couples. He kissed her hair and sat down next to her on the sofa. She grabbed his hand and squeezed it softly.

"You did a good job tonight. I am proud of you."

He searched her eyes, looking for a glimmer of sarcasm but couldn't find any.

"Really? You mean it?"

She nodded and lifted her glass of wine.

"Cheers," she said. "You're a good, honest cop. I'm glad to know you. It does slightly change my perspective on power and authority, I must admit."

"You mean I am turning you into a conservative?" he asked, smiling.

"In your dreams, poppa. But seriously, you did a good job tonight. It's also true that Sheryl was nice with you—she didn't try to claw you too badly. I've seen bloodbaths on this show."

Ratner sighed. "Yeah, I know. I'm sure Rust or some of his cronies will say something about that tomorrow."

"Oh, they already have," Laura said, jumping up. "Rust wrote something on Facebook. Like "It was obvious that Sheryl Boncoeur is Maggie Delgado's best friend by the way she avoided asking City Commissioner Georg Ratner all the right questions." You can check it out yourself. It was on the news."

Ratner shrugged. "Don't need to. Politics bore me."

"I know. They always have. I still wonder what attracted me to such a lackey of power."

"My exceptional good looks, I guess."

"I can't see any other reason."

They exchanged a quick kiss. He smelled her skin for a fraction of a second. A good warmth filled his chest. Happiness was definitely based on the alliance of opposites.

X. THE WHEEL OF FORTUNE

The Wheel of Fortune: Inviting friends over for a costume party. Cloudy sky with blue patches. Blue sky with puffy clouds. The possibilities of a round table. A desire for graffiti. Remember to bring the books back to the library. An unexpected guest.

1

Ratner unzipped the large file Lieutenant Marvin Bailey from the Technical Department had sent him and frowned as he saw the collection of folders appearing on his screen. He opened one and sighed. There were pages and pages of spreadsheets, with tiny columns, names and numbers. He looked up Lacroix's email and forwarded him the zip file, explaining what it was. It was his turf, after all.

His cell phone buzzed and he answered.

"Georg?"

He recognized Sheryl Boncoeur's voice. "Hi, Sheryl."

"I just wanted to thank you for last evening. You were terrific."

"Well, thank *you* for not murdering me in front of the audience."

"Well, I did try to, but you were too dodgy."

They laughed.

"I am having a cocktail party–slash–support event for Maggie Delgado next Saturday evening. You and Laura are officially invited."

"You know Laura won't vote for Delgado," the city commissioner said.

"Even after a few gin and tonics?" Sheryl joked.

Laura and Sheryl had met a couple of times, and Georg knew the two women respected each other—for the same reasons. They were both strong-headed, beautiful and unafraid. It had almost cost Sheryl her life as a young reporter during the South-East China war, and Laura her job, more than once.

"I'll ask her if she wants to come."

"But I can count on you, right? Manny Povero will be there."

"Oh good. I haven't seen him in a long time. He's into politics now?"

He and Povero had shared an art history class when they were in college. They were both into the punk scene and had become close friends. They had followed each other's careers' twists and turns, never losing contact, although they had seen less of each other in the past few years. Povero had gradually become Babylon's most famous artist and Ratner its city commissioner. Busy schedules on both sides.

"Maggie Delgado loves his work and asked the Contemporary Art Museum to commission a piece by him."

"Nice. He sure owes her one, in that case."

"See you Saturday, then?"

"Deal."

Ratner hung up and sighed. He wondered if Laura would join him and he didn't honestly know what answer he would prefer.

2

He called up Lacroix afterward to make sure he had received the email with the zip file. The captain answered that he had and that was now a top priority on his list.

"I don't know how long it will take us to look at all the files, though," Lacroix said. "With all due respect to your position, the cuts are hitting us hard."

"I know," Ratner said. "I know."

He felt like adding something encouraging, but decided against it. His new position did not imply turning him into a hypocrite. At least, not with the people he respected.

"Take your time. Nobody is waiting for this case to be solved. Quite the contrary, maybe."

"I will try my best, Commissioner."

"I don't doubt that."

Ratner hung up and looked at the pile of files on his desk. It seemed to have grown during the night.

3

Ratner decided to leave the office early and visit the National Museum. He felt like seeing some art, something beautiful that remained untouched by greed, politics and violence. Well, in times of peace, at least. Which didn't last, as everybody well knew but pretended to ignore.

4

Once he had walked past the imposing entrance doors of the museum, Ratner hurried toward the Egyptian antiquities section. He stopped in front of what he wanted to see, a granite sarcophagus decorated with the slender figure of a woman arching over a man lying on the ground, her sides decorated with stars. It was Nūt, the Egyptian goddess of the sky.

She had visited him the first time in a dream while he was investigating the Cartoon Killer, way back when, and had showed him important clues. As a cop, Ratner was obsessed with rational thoughts, scientific proofs and nonbiased ethical decisions. As a man, he kept all the doors open, refusing to go through any, but welcoming whoever or whatever came to him through them. As he used to say in private: "All gods and goddesses are welcome in my house, as long as they don't start a fight."

Since that first dream, he often addressed the goddess in his thoughts, on familiar terms. She helped him focus, he felt, and, paradoxically maybe, remain rational when working on a case. One of his good friends, the writer Lee Jones, had a similar experience. He had met the Greek god Hermes in a dream, who had helped him out of a difficult situation. After the dramatic episode was over, Lee began seeing the god everywhere, trying to decode every little insignificant event or encounter as if they were hidden clues. Hermes finally reappeared to him, again in a dream, and put a hand on his shoulder, shaking his head. "Remember, my friend, that not everything is a sign." Ratner had never forgotten this story and quoted it often. Even the gods were rational, in their own tricky way.

He looked for a long time at the beautiful silhouette of Nūt, taking in the peace she radiated. The first time he had dreamed of her, Valentino was his young colleague. They even had an argument about the validity of dreams in an investigation. The rational poet against the mystical cop. They had laughed about that later. Much later, to be honest. Ratner felt a deep sadness weigh on his shoulders.

Going to see Nūt was also his way of paying homage to Valentino's memory, he suddenly realized. He wasn't here to promise his old sidekick that he would catch his killer, that justice would prevail and all that crap, but to hold him close, for a few minutes, in his thoughts. Just that. Yes. Precisely, just that. To dedicate some of his precious time to the sole remembrance of a deceased friend, before the memories began to dissolve into still pictures and anecdotes.

5

Ratner grabbed a paper on his way home. There were twin pictures of Delgado and Rust on the front page, both looking angry. The two candidates were shoulder to shoulder in the last polls, with a slight advance to Delgado. Ratner knew better than to trust figures. They changed with the wind, and you never knew in what direction it would blow next. Rust worried him, though, he had to admit. Not because he would lose his position and certainly be replaced by Thomsen, but because the fragile balance the world had maintained thanks to Delgado in the past four years might be compromised.

The Western Alliance was now on talking terms with the Chinese Federation, New Samarqand, New Moscow and the usual collection of enemy cities. It was a cold peace, sure, but at least not a cold war. Rust would certainly change all that, for the worst and only looking at his own interests. His ideology was the ideology of nothing, or of whatever, whichever one preferred. The populism, the cynicism, the *bragadoccio* were only tin instruments, made louder by their emptiness.

The irony was that the voters were willing to elect a corrupt and greedy businessman to end a global economic crisis caused precisely by greed and corruption. Ratner couldn't help shaking his head and smiling to himself as he remembered an old joke: "As Confucius said, only human stupidity can give us an idea of the infinite." Today, however, he wasn't sure it was a joke anymore.

6

Laura hadn't come home yet and Ratner turned on the news channel. Rust materialized on the screen. "Everybody hates us," he was saying to a cheering audience. "It is time to give some of that hate back!" The city commissioner sighed and turned the TV off. He put on some 1960s Polish avant-garde jazz on the stereo and poured himself a whisky, to which he added a splash of water. Sitting down on the sofa, he routinely checked his personal mail on his phone. There was a message from Bailer, who said hello from New Petersburg, and from Sheryl, reminding him to ask Laura about the party Saturday night. There was also a spam with its usually strange title, "Personal Very Urgent Samarqand Embassy." Ratner was about to delete it when the "Samarqand Embassy" bit suddenly intrigued him. He had never received spam with such a reference before. He decided to open it and frowned as he began reading. It seemed to be official alright and not at all a spam.

It was from a certain Inspector General Ali Shakr Bassam from Samarqand. He explained that due to the tensions between his city and New Babylon, he was using the official channel to contact him in order not to arouse unnecessary suspicion on either of them. He had read about Captain Valentino's murder and wanted to exchange some information that could be useful in the investigation. He offered to have a meeting through Skype at some point and gave his email and Skype contact identification, asking Ratner to remember that Samarqand was nine hours ahead.

Laura walked in as Ratner, looking more and more puzzled, finished reading the message.

"What's wrong?" she asked him. "You're all pale. Bad news?"

"Not sure yet. Weird stuff, though."

He held his phone out to show her the message.

"Wow," she said. "This is like being in a Le Carré novel!"

"Indeed," Ratner agreed. "Indeed."

But it sure wasn't as exciting, he thought as Laura walked into the kitchen. More mind-boggling than anything. He heard Laura open the fridge, then close it. Then open it again. Then close it again.

"Georg, should we go out to eat?" she finally shouted through the open door.

He shut off his phone and stood up. Food seemed the only thing that made sense at this very moment. That, and a few stiff drinks.

7

The chilled winter wind slapped their faces as they walked out, blurring their eyes and making the street neons look like colored smudges. Laura slipped her arm under his and he felt the warmth of her breath against his neck and cheek. *Is our story a love story?* Ratner thought. *Is love the center of everything, or is it outside, on the margins, like an endless ocean or limitless sky?* He began to walk faster because he was cold, but the question remained.

8

They had dinner at their favorite Chinese, which was down the block. After they had finished, Laura cracked open her fortune cookie first. It read: *Never wait too long for something good.*

"Do they mean dessert?" she asked. "It's a bit late for that."

Ratner opened his. It said the same thing.

"That's funny!" Laura said. "It's the first time it ever happened! I don't know if it's ominous or disappointing. Should we ask for another one?"

Ratner shook his head, smiling. "I like these," he said. "Everything becomes more mysterious."

"You're right. Let's keep them and frame them, with the date."

On the way home, Laura suddenly stopped walking. Ratner turned toward her, surprised.

"I know what the cookies mean!" she said. "We should have a cat!"

"Or sex," he joked, nudging her.

"Or both," she retorted wryly. "There were two fortune cookies, remember?"

She took his arm and they ambled slowly home in the icy night, their shadows dancing happily in the traffic lights.

9

Arriving early in his office the following morning, Ratner turned on his private cell phone and looked at the Samarqand message again. He wondered if he should tell Flowers about it or not, already knowing it would probably be a bad idea. Jim would freak out, for sure. Being contacted by a Samarqandi official amidst a national election sounded like bad news all over.

It could also be a trap, something one of Rust's warped and evil advisers could have come up with in order to bring down two targets in one blow, namely him and President Delgado. Yes, the email was probably bad news, but at the same time Ratner felt he couldn't let a possible lead go unexploited.

He decided to leave it aside for the moment and think about it later. He picked up Valentino's file again, which he had put on a shelf next to his chair. He reread the murder report, plus the notes he had taken immediately after meeting with Jesse at Le Robespierre. Who was this John Harding, the whistle-blower who had presumably committed suicide? Mysteries within mysteries.

He buzzed Mrs. Gardiner in, and looked for his cigarettes. There were only two left in the package.

"Yes, Commissioner?"

"I would like you to get me the file of a man who committed suicide about a month ago. His name was John Harding."

He gave her the general info and spelled out Harding's name.

"I'm on it!" she said, with a mock military salute, then slammed her heels together and walked out.

I really like this woman, Ratner thought, lighting a cigarette.

10

Later that night, Laura snoring next to him, Ratner picked up his cell phone and wrote a short message to Inspector General Ali Shakr Bassam, agreeing to Skype with him at his convenience. Life was much more interesting when it was dangerous, after all.

XI. JUSTICE

Justice: A passion for red. Sitting in an uncomfortable chair. Thinking about joining Weight Watchers. A powerful imbecile. Wishing for a new hat. Preparing for a violent revolution.

1

Ratner was finishing a well-deserved cigarette after a hard morning's workload when the door of his office suddenly opened and DA Flowers walked in.

"Jim!" the city commissioner said. "Why don't you just come on in!"

Flowers didn't acknowledge the joke and simply stood there while Mrs. Gardiner cautiously shut the door behind him.

"What's going on? I can recognize trouble when I see it," Ratner said, walking back to his desk.

"There's been a death linked with Synth last night," Flowers said, not moving.

"Uh oh," Ratner said, shaking his head. "Not good."

"Rust is already tweeting about it."

"Of course he is. Are we sure Synth caused the death?"

Flowers shrugged. "The victim's friends saw him buy some Synth at a party, then later the guy jumped from the sixteenth floor. There was definitely Synth in his blood. The link is easy to make."

Ratner nodded pensively. "Does the media know?"

"What do you think?" Flowers snapped back sarcastically.

Thank God it didn't happen before Sheryl's show, the city commissioner thought. *She would have crucified me.*

"Of course. Stupid question, sorry."

"Tchebick sent me to kick your ass, as you can probably guess," Flowers said, avoiding looking Ratner in the eye.

"Of course," Ratner repeated, feeling like a parrot or a stupid talking doll.

"I'm sorry, Georg, because I know you're doing everything you can. But Tchebick and Delgado want results as soon as possible."

The city commissioner looked for his cigarettes on the desk and took one out of the package. "I can't arrest people at random, Jim. You know that. We have nothing. Only small dealers who are buying from other small dealers who are buying from we don't know who!"

Flowers nodded. "I'm only the messenger, Georg."

"And they know I would never shoot you," said Ratner.

They laughed grimly and the DA walked out, leaving the door open behind him. Ratner saw Mrs. Gardiner's face peeking in. He waved at her as she closed the door. He put the unlit cigarette back in the package.

2

"Thank you for agreeing to meet up for this hasty meeting," Ratner said, walking into the conference room of the Narcotics Department.

He shook Captain Jenkins's hand and those of three other officers, one male and two female, all in plain clothes.

"Is that your entire team?" the city commissioner asked Jenkins.

The captain nodded. "Yep. That's all we could spare. Synth hasn't been a high priority, until very recently. We have more detectives dealing with opiate derivatives trafficking, but they are all submerged by their work. Already working overtime without a chance of ever getting their bonuses paid or extra vacation days, if you get my drift."

Ratner got the allusion and nodded sadly. "I know what you mean. I'll talk to DA Flowers. Now that Synth has become a priority, we need more officers on the case."

One of the two female plain clothes, a black woman with beautiful dreadlocks, shrugged.

"Sure thing. But that will mean pulling officers from other urgent business," Jenkins said.

Ratner sighed. "Listen. I know these are tough times for everybody, but there is not much I personally can do, except make sure we do our job well. Or at least, as good as we can, given the circumstances. I am here, with you and ready to support you all the way."

Jenkins sat on a table and crossed her legs. Her thick red hair looked almost brown in the neon light. "We trust you, Commissioner. You have a good rep. Actually, it surprised many of us you accepted the position. It's a rotten job, I hope you know that."

Ratner smiled. "Yes. I knew that. That's why I took it. I like it when things are difficult."

"Famous last words," Jenkins quipped.

Ratner threw down the morning paper editions he had been carrying under his arm. Most of them had a front page story about the Synth-related death of the previous night: "Synth The Killer Drug," "Protect Your Children From Synth," "A Deadly Recreational Drug," "Youth Commits Suicide After Synth Bad Trip."

"This is the situation this morning," Ratner said. "We don't know yet if Synth is the direct or indirect cause of death, if at all. But the media think they do. And the mayor is breathing down my neck. I need results. Now."

Jenkins crossed her arms over her chest and looked at her officers.

"Okay, so what have we got for the city commissioner? Reese? Latka? Femi?"

The three undercover officers told Ratner basically what he already knew. It seemed that Synth circulated only indirectly, and no dealer they had arrested seemed to have bought it from a larger retailer.

"So, what does that tell us?" Ratner asked, when Femi, the Rasta officer had finished speaking.

Jenkins and the three officers looked at him, clueless.

"It's not a trick question," Ratner said. "You are all experienced cops and have worked in the streets for years now. Think hard."

Reese, the other female officer, a redhead like Jenkins, raised her hand as if she was in class.

"I don't know, but maybe . . . there *isn't* any large retailer?"

"Yes, exactly," Ratner said. "And what does that mean, for us?"

"That we have to understand how the drug comes into this city, and what channels it uses to appear on the market," Jenkins answered.

"Exactly," Ratner agreed. "We have to think creatively. Synth seems to come out of nowhere, yet it is almost everywhere. Actually, maybe we should focus on that: the media say it's everywhere, but is it really? Is it a cheap drug?"

Latka, the male officer with dark mediterranean features, shrugged. "It's sold between fifteen and twenty-five dollars per pill. Not too expensive, but definitely not cheap either."

"How widely spread is it? What is your estimation?" Ratner asked.

"We don't exactly know," Reese said. "Lots of people talk about it. It's a fashionable drug and some communities seem particularly fond of it, like artists, musicians, students and, some say, radical political activists. And it's true that most of the dealers we've caught gravitated within or around these circles."

"But the usual junkies and meth heads keep to the good old stuff," Jenkins chipped in. "Heroin, cocaine and methamphetamine are still the most popular drugs around. I would estimate Synth is an 'elite' drug, if that makes sense."

Ratner scratched his head. "Yes, that makes very good sense. If it circulates among wealthy, cultured young people with middle- or upper-class parents, it precisely threatens our 'elites.' Hence the *real* danger."

"You're right," Jenkins agreed. "We haven't connected any serious crime or even violence related to Synth yet. That death yesterday is completely new. Maybe a new type of Synth? More dangerous?"

Ratner shrugged. "Maybe. I guess it's irrelevant, as the media and our politicians don't care. For them, Synth is Synth and has to be wiped out. Any info about the places where the dealers were arrested that we can use?"

Jenkins made a dubious face and pointed at a map of the city that was pinned on the wall. "You can see it yourself. It's all over the city, but only ten to twenty pills each time. Never more. Very peculiar."

"Maybe it's a strategy," Ratner said. "Maybe it's deliberate."

Officer Femi frowned. "How do you mean?"

Ratner crossed his arms. "If you don't want to attract attention, you are going to sell the drug in limited quantity only."

"Yeah, but what about the profit?" Jenkins asked. "Small quantities equal small profit. No drug dealer is interested in small profit."

"Right," the city commissioner agreed. "Unless it isn't really a market drug, but more like an experiment or something."

"How do you mean?" Jenkins asked.

Ratner shook his head. "I'm not sure. It's only a feeling. But imagine someone is studying the effects of the drug in our city, or trying to discreetly manipulate society through its elites, or whatever . . . I must sound paranoid, but there is definitely something that doesn't add up in the picture."

Jenkins nodded. "I agree with you. You are seeing the drug as a deliberate weapon used against us by a political group, if I understand you correctly?"

"Yes, maybe. It would explain some things. I heard there were communities forming around Synth now, and artistic and musical movements. Like parallel societies within our own. Against our own, maybe not violently, but ideologically."

"But it's not linked with any political movement, like LSD was in the sixties," Officer Latka said.

"True," Ratner conceded "But that might be the trick, you see. No official political agenda and a drug that 'shows you' that our reality sucks—it's a new form of revolutionary subversion, whose only goal is to disrupt our political and social system. It would be genius. The ultimate conspiracy theory: a conspiracy without an obvious political agenda."

"And would those be 'conspirators'?" Jenkins asked.

"That's what we have to find out," Ratner said. "If we find an agenda linked with Synth or something resembling it, we might come closer to the source."

"And where would that agenda be?" Femi asked. "I can't see it anywhere."

"Let's begin with the users—let's try to identify them. The students, the artists, the musicians . . . maybe they have something in common, something we don't see. A contact, a place, a website."

"We can't arrest these people without a good reason," Jenkins said.

"No, you're right. But we can pay a visit to all those who were caught on a possession charge and talk with them. Put some pressure on the network, if there is a network. Not harass them, but you know . . . call them in the station once in a while, for no reason. See what happens. Maybe they'll end up telling us something. Those who are in the loop, that is. If there's a loop, of course."

"That's the question," Jenkins said. "And that's a lot of people and I've got only three officers."

"I'm going to call Flowers as soon as I get out of this meeting," Ratner said. "You'll get a larger team. Promise."

He lifted his hand doing the scout sign. *I have never been a scout*, he thought as he was walking back to his car. *I hope the God of Scouts will help me on this anyway.*

3

In the car's comfortable back seat, Ratner checked his emails on his phone. His heart jumped a little as he saw he had a message from the Inspector General Ali Shakr Bassam from Samarqand. Holding his breath he took a quick look at it. Bassam was suggesting they speak on Sunday evening, at six p.m. New Babylon time. Ratner wrote back that it was fine, and put the phone back in the inside pocket of his coat. He looked through the window at the busy streets. The end of November night had fallen already, turning the city into a shimmering and dark fabric.

XII. THE HANGED MAN

The Hanged Man: Domestic incident. Changing your mind about suicide. Trying to look casual in a ridiculous situation. A sudden idea. Thinking about taking yoga lessons. Remember that whatever the situation, the choice is always yours: it's only a question of angle.

1

"Georg! Laura! I'm so glad you could come!"

Sheryl looked absolutely magnificent in a golden lamé dress which left one of her shoulders uncovered. She kissed them on the cheek and took a step back.

"Laura! You look stunning!"

"Thank you," Laura said, slightly embarrassed. "You do too."

Laura had chosen to wear a red and dark purple sari-inspired dress, and Ratner agreed with Sheryl: she did look fantastic. While the two women exchanged exclamations and chit-chat, his eyes wandered on the guests crowding Sheryl's mansion in clusters of various sizes, colors and conversation volume. He recognized Mayor Tchebick's large bald Mussolini head bobbing up and down in a sea of sponsors and lobbyists. Jim Flowers stood near the bar and buffet table talking with a famous actor. A slow moving caravan of secret service agents—all ironically immediately recognizable with their dark glasses, earsnails and black suits—indicated the presence of President Delgado. He also caught a few famous faces waving at Sheryl, sailing past like beautiful Italian designed warships accompanied by their flotilla of admirers.

He finally spotted his old friend, the artist Manny Povero, surrounded by what he supposed were gallery owners and rich collectors. Excusing himself, the city commissioner left Sheryl in order to join Povero, Laura at his arm.

A journalist and her crew filmed them as they passed by, complimenting Laura on her dress. Ratner felt her push his arm so they would walk away faster.

As they made their way through the large hall, a large man with a white suit suddenly left Tchebick's group and grabbed his arm.

"Commissioner! Leon Shultz, New Babylonian Tobacco Company. I just wanted to tell you we are very honored to be your sponsor."

Ratner nodded and shook the extended had, adorned with a heavy gold ring.

"I hope they will send us a carton of Navy Cuts for Christmas," Laura whispered in his ear as they walked away.

2

Ratner grabbed two champagne glasses from the tray of a passing waitress. He gave one to Laura, and they approached the little group surrounding Manny Povero.

"Van Gogh died poor," Ratner said, getting insulted glances from Manny's entourage. "And so did Gauguin."

"But Cézanne and Monet were rich bastards," Povero answered, smiling.

"How goes it, my painter friend?"

"As you can see," the artist answered, indicating his admiring cronies with a large gesture.

"He's doing too well," Amelia, Povero's wife, interjected, joining the group with a glass of wine. "He's getting fat and pretentious."

Ratner noticed some silent eye-rolling among the painter's admirers.

"I think this is true for both of them," Laura agreed, gently patting the city commissioner's arm.

A press photographer stopped and took a couple of pictures of the group. Ratner and Povero posed together, looking serious.

"A smile?" the photographer asked.

"No," they answered in unison.

And they laughed.

3

Ratner and Povero retreated to a quieter space—one of the side rooms of the mansion—when the other guests moved into the main hall to hear president Maggie Delgado deliver a campaign speech and thank the fundraisers, Sheryl Boncoeur included.

Amelia and Laura joined the audience, out of curiosity more than political fandom. Ratner knew that Laura would vote for the Socialist Revolutionary Party, bringing her total score to 1.1%, and he assumed that Amelia wasn't the voting type—way too original for that kind of triviality.

Sitting on two quite uncomfortable chairs, a half-empty champagne glass in hand, the two friends sighed in unison, scanning the near empty room. Only a drunk couple sat on the other side, not talking to each other and simply staring at their empty glasses.

"I didn't know you were into politics," Ratner jabbed jokingly.

"Right back atcha," Povero countered, smiling.

They raised their glasses and drank a sip.

"Getting old, I guess," Ratner offered, as an excuse.

"Same here. Plus, the Museum of Modern Art has commissioned five paintings for one of their new rooms."

Ratner smiled. "Yeah, I heard. Sheryl told me. Delgado is a big fan of yours, it seems."

"We're living in Roman times, my dear Georg," Povero said, looking for his cigarettes. "Our patrons are all into politics, no matter what their trade is, and we have to accept that if we want to achieve our goals. My dream was to be exhibited in a museum's permanent collection. It is done."

Ratner accepted the cigarette Povero was offering him, and blew out a thin smoke cloud. "Would you have accepted if Rust had been a fan?"

Povero shrugged. "No," he smiled. "I might be a whore, but I still have morals. That guy is a nightmare. I really hope Delgado wins, and not just because she likes my stuff."

"I hear you," Ratner said. "I hear you."

Povero downed his champagne and smacked his lips. "I think Delgado's finished her speech," he said, getting up. "The way to the bar must be open again. The only way to stand these hard times is to get really drunk on somebody else's champagne."

4

Ratner was suffering under the shower. He had woken up with a bad hangover and made a mental note to remember that expensive bubbles didn't agree with him. The positive thing was that Laura, surprisingly, had enjoyed herself, chatting with Amelia and Sheryl for the most part of the evening. She even exchanged a few words with Maggie Delgado and managed to conceal her political opinions. He was glad to have seen Povero again and to realize they still were on the same wavelength. He had promised to visit him at his studio some time soon, and he was planning on holding to his word.

He had also run into another old friend, the bestselling writer Lee Jones, who was already too drunk to have a normal conversation. They had fun, though, until Lee tried to score hoops with olives in the passing ladies' cleavages. He was politely escorted out by Secret Service guys with half-smiles on their faces. They knew they were throwing out a harmless clown. What they probably didn't know was that he was one of the best writers of his generation. But then again, even if they had known this, they would have dragged him out all the same, maybe even more enthusiastically.

5

Ratner put down the newspaper he had been reading, while stretched out comfortably on the sofa, and massaged his tired, hungover eyes. Laura was preparing her classes in the grim afternoon of the first day of December, and he could smell her cup of instant coffee. Streaming from his telephone, new avant-garde industrial jazz filled the room with its strange and exotic rhythms. His mind played like an old vinyl, scratching and skipping tracks.

Should I resign? he was thinking. *Should I quit the sinking ship before it's too late and I've lost all my honor and credibility? Love the way Laura is concentrating, doing her best for these poor kids, trying to make their lives a little bit less miserable. Maybe I should read a book, that would keep me from thinking stupid thoughts. But if I resigned, then Thomsen would probably replace me, and that would be the end of everything. Povero looked good. Happy for him. His works definitely belong in a museum. At least, he's not a sorry wannabe. The real thing, like that poor Lee.* He chuckled out loud, making Laura turn her head.

"What's on your mind?" she asked, pressing the tip of her pen against her lovely lower lip.

"Lee Jones," Ratner answered. "I feel sorry for him, about last night."

Laura nodded, putting down her pen. "Well, you know him," she said, grabbing her mug of coffee. "He loves to provoke when he's drunk."

"We should invite him for dinner soon," Ratner said. "We could also have Povero and Amelia that same evening."

Laura made a mock surprised face. "Anything wrong, darling? Suddenly feel the need of some human company?"

Ratner grunted, acknowledging the irony. "Must be the winter blues getting to me," he said. "I think I need a drink. It's almost six p.m. now. I'm allowed."

"Fix one for me too, then," Laura said, stretching on her chair. "I think I blew my brain preparing these activities."

Ratner got up and fixed two whiskies in the kitchen. He sat at the table with Laura and put down one of the glasses in front of her.

"Did I tell you Marian might be leaving us?" she said.

Marian was the head of the school where Laura taught. A tough, sharp and honest woman, she was one of the few people in this world Laura truly respected.

"No. Really? Why?"

"Because she is tired of having to fire people because of budget cuts, that's why. The economy is getting in better shape day after day, yet we're still destroying all the city's social services. I'm sure it's the same with the police, right?"

Ratner emitted a noncommittal grunt. He didn't feel like discussing politics with a hangover. His phone suddenly rang. It was the Skype tone and he remembered his scheduled meeting with Inspector General Ali Shakr Bassam from Samarqand.

"Shit!" he mumbled, jumping to his feet and hurrying into the bedroom. "Don't come in!" he shouted to Laura as he shut the door."It's an important call!"

And maybe a dangerous one, he thought, as he swiped the green button with the phone symbol.

6

Inspector General Ali Shakr Bassam was sitting at his home, a beautiful woven carpet hanging behind him. Probably in his mid-fifties, the man had a nice round face decorated with a thick black mustache. His hair was black too, combed backward with streaks of white, and he was wearing a white shirt. *The face of an enemy,* Ratner thought, *if we were in some kind of spy flick.*

"Hello!" Shakr Bassam said tentatively."Hello, hello! Can you hear me? Can you see me?"

He waved a hand, as if he was saying goodbye.

Ratner refrained from waving back, feeling a little self-conscious.

"Yes, everything is fine."

"You can call me Ali," the jovial man said.

"You can call me Georg," Ratner answered politely.

"Yes, that will be more simple. I am glad you accepted to talk to me."

"Of course."

"I have learned with great regret that one of your best poets, Jesse Valentino, was assassinated a few weeks ago."

Ratner nodded, noncommittal but nevertheless suddenly intrigued.

"He was truly an exceptional voice. I have followed him for some years now. A true loss for us all."

"Indeed," Ratner said dryly.

"I also know that you were friends."

Ratner was now truly surprised. Samarqandi intelligence had a solid reputation, but were they really that good? Had they spied their talk at Le Robespierre? Were they following Valentino? And if so, why?

"Really?" Ratner said. "How do you know that, if I may ask?"

"He dedicated a series of poems to you. It's on his website. You must have felt very honored."

"Of course," Ratner lied. *The simplest solution is always the right solution,* he remembered, blushing lightly.

"May I ask what department you are working in, Inspector General?"

"Call me Ali, please. Homicide. Just like you. Sorry, I forgot to mention that."

"Why are you so interested in Captain Valentino's murder?"

Shakr Bassam joined his hands in front of his face, as if he were going to pray. "You see, Valentino is not the only internationally recognized poet recently murdered. It happened here also, a few months back. Olgeÿ Tazar. One of our most famous poets. You may have heard about it."

Ratner shook his head. "No, sorry."

"And Valérie Bizet in New Belleville, just last week. Ricardo Santos in New Buenos Aires, Natalia Atanasov in New Moscow. All in the past year, all political poets and writers."

Ratner frowned. "You think these murders are related?"

"Maybe not in the way you think, but yes, I do."

"How do you mean 'not in the way I think'?"

Shakr Bassam had a little laugh. "You're a cop, like me, Georg. If I say these murders are related, you will probably think of some international conspiracy, or a secret political group—something similar. Well, it is and it isn't. It's more complicated than that."

Ratner scratched his cheek and reminded himself he should shave soon. "Go on," he said.

"Have you ever heard of the Egregorians?" Shakr Bassam asked.

"No, never. What are they?"

"A secret group. Very, very secret, actually. That's why you've never heard of them."

Ratner wondered where this conversation was leading. He felt trapped in a labyrinth that grew weirder with each step he took.

"Are they the bad guys you're thinking of?"

The Inspector General laughed again. It was a nice laugh, warm and deep. "No, no! On the contrary, they're the good guys."

Ratner was completely confused now. "How do you mean? Who are they?"

Shakr Bassam moved closer to the camera. "I am going to tell you a very important secret, because I trust you. Actually, I am going to put my life in your hands, because if anybody here learns about this, you will never see me again. You are hanged for much less in this city, you know."

Ratner remained silent, remembering Valentino's face when Ratner had told him they should follow dreams in order to catch the Cartoon Killer. It had actually worked as the goddess Nūt had shown Ratner an essential clue in one of his dreams, but Valentino had never mentioned it again. Right here, right now, Ratner felt *exactly* like Valentino must have felt.

"I am an Egregorian," Ali Shakr Bassam resumed. "Do you know what an *égrégore* is, Georg?"

"No, I actually don't," Ratner admitted.

"To make it simple, let's say it's a collective thought that becomes a real entity. If a sufficient number of people believe in or desire the same thing, it can come to life. Gods are égrégores. War is an égrégore. Ideologies are égrégores. They only last as long there are people believing enough in them, but as you can see throughout history, they can do a lot of damage."

"Are all égrégores bad? You mentioned war—what about peace? Can't it become an égrégore too?"

"Sometimes . . . sometimes it can, yes," Shakr Bassam admitted. "But only when war has become weak, and generally, it doesn't last very long. Human desires are usually very violent."

"So what do you guys do?" the city commissioner asked, genuinely interested this time. "Create them by yourselves? Try to manipulate them? I thought you were the good guys."

"No, no, we don't create them at all. We study them, we fight them, but most important of all, we try to predict them."

"Predict them?"

"Yes. That's why I contacted you."

"I don't understand."

The Inspector General smiled and shook his head. "No, of course you don't. You can't. Let me enlighten you the best I can. You have recently seen a rise of bad vibrations in politics these past years, no? In Viborg City, New Belleville, here in New Samarqand, and now in New Babylon. Rust is an embodiment of this crisis for you, if you see what I mean."

"Do you mean Rust is an égrégore?" Ratner couldn't believe he was asking such a question. His dream encounters with the goddess Nūt seemed childplay compared to this.

"No, but he definitely participates in creating one. And a very bad one. If New Babylon manages to create an égrégore, with the city-state's immense power, it will be a terrifying thing."

The city commissioner frowned. "What does Valentino's murder have to do with this?"

Shakr Bassam pursed his lips. "A sign that an égrégore is about to be born is usually when poets, writers and artists are assassinated. Or completely ignored, while meaningless puppets are worshiped. The Egregorian Society was founded in 1934, in Germany, right after the first book *auto-da-fé* took place. The founders felt that something very, very bad was happening, and they were right. So they decided to create the society to monitor these monsters and protect what the monsters longed to destroy: culture—as in *free* culture, of course. They began searching history in order to find links between the murder or persecution of writers and artists, and catastrophic times. Socrates, Hypatia, Lermontov, Garcia Lorca, Neruda—just a few names on their list—their deaths always announced darker times. Valentino has just been added to that long list."

"I still don't see what I can do," Ratner said drily.

He was feeling irritated now. All of this was nonsense.

"It's very simple," said Shakr Bassam. "Try to find a political connection to Valentino's killer. If there is one, then we are right and we have to protect other writers of your city."

"We have no idea who the killer is, to be honest. It seems that he was mugged and murdered. Nothing political in this."

The Inspector General smiled like a grown-up smiles to a small child.

"Hmmm. Are you sure? There was nothing strange about this murder? Something missing, something that the criminal had no reason to take?"

Ratner suddenly thought of Valentino's notebook, the one in which he wrote down his poems. "Well, I don't know. Maybe."

"Another clue is to check with his publisher. Sometimes they are attacked too."

"I will do that, thank you, Inspector General."

"Call me Ali. Please keep me posted. It is very important for our organization—in case we have to set up a *résistance* network against this possible upcoming *égrégore*. It is still weak for now, uncertain if you will. It can be defeated."

"Yes, yes, of course, I will," Ratner promised, half-heartedly.

He turned off his phone and looked at it for a while, letting his thoughts settle down like mud in water.

The door opened and Laura's joyous face appeared.

"I heard you were finished in there. Gin and tonic?"

"You bet," Ratner said.

Nothing better than cheap bubbles to clear the mud.

7

Later that night, Ratner stared at the ceiling, incapable of falling asleep. Was the world spinning out of control, all of a sudden, or was he just caught in his own whirlwind? The ceiling reminded him of the granite lid of an Egyptian tomb, heavy, mysterious, ominous. The lights coming from the street and the traffic drew ephemeral hieroglyphs he couldn't decipher. He fell asleep reluctantly, like a prisoner dragged to his execution.

8

The woman was standing by the open window of the room, her dark silhouette clearly visible on the background of a blinding blue sky. It looked like daytime, but the moon shone in the middle of the window, full, silver and gorgeous. The walls were made of black stone, glittering faintly in the moonlight. The smell of a heady perfume pervaded the atmosphere. She slowly turned around, her naked body covered with what looked like stardust. Ratner recognized his old friend Nūt, the Egyptian goddess of the sky and his occasional detective sidekick.

"So, it seems you need me again, Georg," she said maliciously, her voice deep and soft, like a harp played by the wind.

"Weeell . . ." Ratner began.

"Tsk, tsk, tsk, Georg," Nūt said. "You know that I know. You called me and I am here. Actually, to be honest, I know that you didn't *realize* you were calling me, but I felt it when you went to see me at the museum."

"Probably . . ." the city commissioner said, half-convinced.

"But you should also know I cannot help you, Georg. Not the way you would want me to, anyway."

Georg shifted the weight on his legs and realized he was naked too. It didn't shock him though. Nothing was ever shocking with Nūt. He remained silent, knowing the goddess had not finished her speech.

"I can only offer you comfort, not help. The times are dark and murky, and I cannot see through them. But I am here for you, this you should know. If I see anything, I will let you know immediately. I will not let you down. I promise. But you have to walk this world carefully, Georg, and always think twice. Two is the magic number here, but one and one, not one plus one. This is very important to understand. Do you understand, my dear friend?"

Georg nodded. "I understand that I will understand at some point," he said.

"That is what I hope, and you have to remember. Balance is always an unsatisfactory solution, and the weights are uneven. But in the end, it is what makes justice prevail, even when it does not look like justice. I have spoken."

She smiled, lifted her hand, opened her palm and blew him a silent kiss. Ratner thought he saw stars floating his way like silver rose petals.

XIII. DEATH

Death: Going to the horse races. A visit to the family. Enjoying the sunset knowing there will be a sunrise. A nostalgia for the middle-ages. The desire to become an anarchist gardener. The possibility of a possibility. A distrust for bishops.

1

Ratner felt strangely refreshed as he walked into his office, and it was all the more striking because it was a Monday. He always felt good after meeting Nūt in his dreams. Maybe she was just an égrégore as Ali Shakr Bassam had named such apparitions, a figment of his imagination; but she had nonetheless always helped him many times before and given him good advice, even if he didn't always completely understand it at the time. Like last night.

He went to the window and looked at the concrete and glass monster slowly wake up in the dark morning. He could make out the river Styx by the large dark gap that cut the city in two. It was as dark as Nūt's room and as beautiful and mysterious. All cities were tombs, after all, and New Babylon maybe even more so than others.

There was a knock on the door that made him turn his head. Mrs. Gardiner walked in and put a thin file on his desk.

"This is the Harding file you asked for a few days ago," she explained. "It took a little while to get access to it. Red tape and all that, you know."

"Thank you very much," the city commissioner said, moving back to his desk.

The Harding file was indeed thin, as the autopsy record was missing. He scanned the pictures of the crime scene, which didn't tell him much. It indeed looked like a suicide, but then professional killers were well paid precisely because they were professionals.

He opened an A4 size envelope. It was the thickest document of the whole file, and it wasn't much more than twenty-five pages. It contained various interviews of the victim's friends and family members. They all basically said the same thing: that Harding was neither a pervert nor suicidal. His girlfriend's interview was especially interesting to Ratner, as she mentioned Harding's interest in Green Star coming from his militant environmentalist background. A lead like any other and most probably a dead-end, but it was his job to make sure.

He dialed the cell phone number she had given the detectives. After two short rings she answered and Ratner declined his identity.

"Yes? What can I do for you?"

Her tone was sharp, dismissive. *Not a lover of the Force*, Ratner thought. He explained that he had taken an interest in her boyfriend's death and wanted to ask her a few questions.

"I already answered your colleagues. They didn't sound too interested at the time."

"I am interested. Seriously."

"Really? You don't think it's a suicide either?"

Her tone of voice had changed. *Opening up,* Ratner thought. *Good.*

"No, I actually don't. But you have to know that the case is officially closed. I can't reopen it, unless I have evidence. And I have none so far. Some things don't add up and I do want to take a closer look. But . . ." he hesitated, "but it's not official. It's just me. I have no leverage here. So it has to remain strictly between us, do you understand? Like I never called you and you never answered me."

There was a short silence at the other end. "Am I in danger? Can this be dangerous?"

"No, I don't think so. It can be dangerous for my career if some people learn that I talked to you, that's all. Some people who don't want the truth to come out."

"Will it?"

"Sorry?"

"The truth. Will it come out, do you think?"

"Eventually," the city commissioner answered, diplomatically. "That's why I want to ask you some questions."

Another short silence. "Okay. Shoot."

"You said in your interview that John had joined Green Star because he was a dedicated environmentalist. Can you be a little more precise?"

"Yes, of course. We met in the office of Back To Earth, you know, the organization. I still work there, incidentally. John was a great asset for us. Enthusiastic, dedicated, honest. When we targeted Green Star, he was all for it. Very happy about his mission."

"Excuse me, I don't get this. How do you mean, 'targeted'?"

"Do you know Back To Earth, Commissioner?"

Ratner scratched his cheek. "Well, I know it's an environmental organization, a little bit like Greenpeace, right?"

"Wrong. We're not at all like Greenpeace. We're a legal organization, testing so-called 'green' corporations and businesses from the inside to verify their dedication. After two years of investigation, we give out an evaluation report and a rating: three earths, clean; two earths, could be better; one earth, not good; black earth, bullshit. John had been employed by Green Star for about eight months when he died."

Ratner felt his brain cells connect in new ways.

"Really? Did you tell the detectives about this?"

"Yes, I did."

Ratner looked at the report on his desk. Nothing of it was written down. Erased? Rewritten?

"Why didn't your organization, Back To Earth, say anything? I mean, if there was a possibility John was murdered, they should look into it, right?"

"We discussed it. We decided not to say anything and try to infiltrate Green Star again as soon as possible. We didn't want them to be suspicious."

Realpolitik, Georg thought. These people were pragmatists. Therefore dangerous, to some.

"Of course, I understand," Ratner said. "Is anyone there now?"

"No, not yet. They're not hiring at the moment."

"Good," Georg said. "Better stay low for a while anyway."

"I guess so," the girl said. "I hope you find what you're looking for. I loved John."

"I hope so too," Ratner said, sincerely.

He thought of Harding and Valentino as he put down the phone. What had they gotten into? What had they come across that had cost them their lives?

He logged on to Green Star's website. It was flashy and beautifully designed. Lots of earth-friendly awards and logos, but nothing from Back To Earth. On the upper right corner there was a video with Sam Rosen, the CEO of the company. Nice-looking guy, with a Robert Redford hairdo and blond dye, wearing a casual jean shirt opened on graying chest fur.

"You love coffee," he was saying as he walked in the middle of a field that obviously wasn't a coffee plantation, "but you also love the idea of enjoying it fully, without thinking about the moral issues that might come with the nice cup you're drinking. Here, at Green Star, we value—" *Bla, bla, bla*, thought Georg as he stopped the short film.

Ratner looked at the still image of Sam Rosen. Was this guy a cold-blooded killer? Could this charming man have ordered the murder of one of his executives? Ratner's experience told him *of course*, but his gut feeling remained vague. He needed to dig deeper, to get more info about the man. He noted that down on his mental to-do list and lit a cigarette. Everything in its time—but politics couldn't wait.

He looked at the address he had written on a post-it and he mockingly felt for his imaginary colts and silver star. He was a man with a mission, after all. The citizens deserved his protection, even if they hadn't really asked for it—but the authorities had decided that Synth was a danger to them, and it had to be taken care of. He grabbed his coat, a cigarette hanging from his lower lip. From sheriff to PI Marlowe. A morning of impersonations.

2

Synth Records was, unsurprisingly, located in one of those newly created "Synth communes" that the media loved to describe as lairs of free sex, free drugs and subversive politics. All their references pointed back at the late 1960s, both as click-bait and just because they couldn't really understand what was going on—as always.

Historical approximations and deformations were a constant and annoying characteristic of the mainstream media and that's why Ratner distrusted them with a vengeance. He was actually glad his investigation had taken him out to see reality, away from the usual narratives and judgment. He was a cop, and a cop had to know his shit—the real shit, not the plastic thing sold in novelty shops.

The commune was located in a huge six-story brown brick building, probably squatted (he would have to check it out), covered with graffiti art that was arguably supposed to express the effects of Synth. Actually, to be honest and to his surprise, it was more art than graffiti. Perhaps even beautiful in some sort of strange way.

The door was open—or rather, there was no door—and he walked into an immaculate white hall and saw a panel covered with indications. The kindergarten and the cafeteria were on the ground floor, the assembly room and the chill room on the second floor, and Synth Records on the third. Ratner guessed the rest were apartments. A colorful poster in cool jazzy fifties graphics on the opposite wall said that this week would be "Beatnik Week," whatever that meant.

A young woman walked out, briefly looking at him. She was dressed normally, in jeans and a thick coat. Only a small purple dot tattooed on her forehead might have indicated some "hippiness" or "Synthness" in her. But Georg didn't know if it was just a personal tattoo or a recognition mark among Synthers. He would have to ask.

Walking up the chilly concrete stairs, the city commissioner realized how little he actually knew about Synth, Synthers and the Synth subculture. All his info basically came from the media and the general rumors, but he had no more documentation than that. He felt somewhat both vulnerable and naive, like a rookie on his first mission. The thought made him smile. A wrinkled, bone-aching and gray-haired rookie, but then again it was never too late to start from scratch.

3

The door to Synth Records was half-open, but Ratner politely knocked all the same. A small silhouette appeared, and he recognized Warren Deich, the DAO music producer.

"Yes?" the short man said. He was wearing a loose beige sweater, creased black pants and an open collared white shirt.

Ratner was surprised to see how short he was. From the video he had seen, he had imagined a tall, slender man, with elegant gestures and he was confronted by what could have been a good impersonation of a Tolkien dwarf, if Tolkien dwarves had looked intellectual and wore 1960s Colonel Sanders glasses.

"City Commissioner Ratner," he showed Deich his badge. "I would like to talk to you."

Deich frowned. "You have a warrant?"

Ratner smiled. "You're not under arrest. It's just a talk. I would like to know more about DAO and . . . stuff."

Deich's frown morphed into surprised eyebrows. "DAO? Seriously? Why?"

"Weeell . . ." Ratner began. "Let's talk inside, if you don't mind."

"Sure, sure. But it's a mess."

I'm a mess too, Ratner thought as he walked into the studio. *Mess doesn't frighten me.*

The studio was a large loft, with graffiti art decorating the walls. The company's name, *DAO RECORDS*, was beautifully lettered on one side, in psychedelic colors. A few chairs were scattered around. There was an army of laptops crowding long tables, with wires and stuff littering the floor, but apart from that, everything seemed immaculate. *If this is a mess*, Ratner thought, *then the guy must suffer from OCD.* The way Deich moved two chairs precisely in front of each other confirmed his suspicion.

The routine of questions and answers, the city commissioner thought as he grabbed one the of the chairs. *How tragically boring and familiar. If there should ever be a movie about me, it would be a long, endless German black-and-white film with only dialogue.*

Three people were standing around a computer at the farthest end of the loft, all with earphones on. They seemed to be in their mid-twenties and wore hoodies and sports sneakers. Two were black—one a silver bejewelled man, the other a stern-looking woman with red dreadlocks—and the third was a chubby white guy with one gold front tooth. They could have been hip-hoppers, for all Ratner knew.

He politely saluted them from afar, and they answered him awkwardly, probably sensing his copness.

"Plus Equals Minus," Darren said, cryptically.

"Sorry?" Ratner asked, perplexed.

"Plus Equals Minus. The band, you know? You don't listen to the radio?"

Ratner shook his head. "No, too mainstream for me," he explained, with a smile, as he sat down on his chair. "I didn't know DAO was played on the radio."

"Not on all of the stations, but some of them. Not illegal yet," he quipped.

Ratner nodded. "Good. I'm against censorship."

"So, what can I do for you, Commissioner?" Darren asked, pushing his glasses back on his nose. I'm pretty sure you're not here to discuss music."

"Well, actually, yes, I am. In a way," Ratner said, crossing his arms on his chest. "I want to learn more about Synth culture."

"Like the FBI wanted to know more about Hippie culture?"

Ratner smiled. "I see you know your classics. To be honest, yes, something like that. I saw an interview of you on YouTube. Thought it was very interesting. I like music. I love industrial jazz, for example. And I was a metapunk in my youth."

It was Darren's turn to smile. "A metapunk? What the hell is that?"

Ratner shrugged. "Oh, just a short-lived movement in Babylon and Petersburg, some thirty years ago. Bands like No Bird, Lone Grunger and Metatools. Maybe you know them?"

Darren shook his head no.

"Metatools? Fuck, man, they were great. Did you ever see them live?"

Both Ratner and Darren turned their heads toward Plus Equals Minus. It was the black guy who had spoken, his earphones now around his neck.

"Yeah," Ratner said. "A couple of times. I knew Kobe, the lead singer."

"No way, man! I'm jealous." The guy lifted two thumbs up and put his earphones back on.

"I guess I'll have to extend my scope," Darren said. "First time I speak about music with a cop, who on top of that knows bands I never heard of."

"Never take anything for granted, I guess," Ratner philosophized. "My personal motto."

The producer nodded and fiddled with his glasses again. "So, what are you interested in knowing?" he asked.

"Why is Synth such a popular drug? What does it do? And what is a 'Synth Community' like this one?"

"Synth is not a popular drug, it is a drug for the people, Commissioner," Darren explained, this time very serious."It allows us to see beyond the social and political walls artificially constructed by the Power, with a big *P*."

"Reality, you mean?" Ratner asked, without intended irony.

"Whatever you want to call it, yes. You see, Synth doesn't control you, you control it. It helps you build your own environment. You can turn it on and off anytime you want. That's why it's so great. You can live a completely different life within the frame of this imposed reality."

"And why do you create communes if it's such a personal experience?"

"Because if you are tuned right, you can share the same visions. Or you can decide to share the same visions."

"Really?" Ratner was skeptical.

He then remembered the poster in the hall downstairs. "That 'Beatnik Week' poster, is that what it's about? You are all living in the 1950s for a week?"

Darren nodded. "Exactly."

"Sounds like Cosplay to me, without the costumes."

"Well, that's because you don't *see* the costumes. We do."

Ratner scratched his cheek and realized he hadn't shaved this morning. "How can you 'share' a vision?" he said. "Sounds like telepathy to me. And, to be honest, I don't believe in telepathy. Or a shared hallucination."

Darren laughed dryly. "This is such a typical question, man! You need to define things as you've learned them. Synth makes you unlearn and relearn. It destroys and rebuilds."

"That's what DAO does too, with music?"

"Yes, absolutely. Do you want to hear?"

"Sure."

Darren got up from his chair and went to talk to the three members of Plus Equals Minus. He seemed minuscule compared to the musicians, but there wasn't anything funny about this situation—on the contrary, everything seemed harmonious, flowing, beautiful even. Then Ratner understood. Respect. From all sides. If Synth did also create that, then he saw an even greater danger for society indeed.

The trio nodded and the white guy with the gold tooth fiddled with the computers. A heavy beat filled up the room, but distant, muffled as if it came from a dark forest. Then shiny layers seemed to rise, followed by long, heavy riffs. Ratner felt goosebumps on his forearms. It was both frightening and beautiful, a new sound with a mixture of familiar textures, yet impossible to identify. He imagined the effect while on drugs. Quite a trip, literally.

Darren came back to sit down on his chair while the song was playing, nodding to the riffs. When the number was finished Ratner applauded slowly, lifting a thumb at the trio.

"Impressive," the commissioner told Darren.

"You see, drugs are good for you," the tiny man said, with a wry smile.

"For music, undoubtedly. Speaking of which . . ."

"We're all under arrest," Darren joked grimly.

"No, not yet," Ratner joked back. "I just want to know a couple of things."

"Like the name of my dealer."

"For example."

Darren shook his head. "There are no Synth dealers. Or rather, we are all dealers. It's not a drug for profit. It's a liberation drug. The price is set. You can't sell it for a higher price, or you'll get in trouble."

Ratner ran his fingers through his thinning hair. "That's not what my officers told me. They said Synth pills had a price range."

Darren shrugged. "Bad info."

Ratner pursed his lips. "How is the price set? Who sets it?"

"The community sets it."

"OK, but how?"

Darren smiled. "Come on, I'm not going to tell you that, of course. Even if you arrest me."

Ratner nodded.

The members of Plus Equal Minus walked past. The girl stopped and briefly told Darren they would be back later to work on another track.

"You're a cool cop, man," the black guy said, hitting Ratner's shoulder as he strolled by him.

"Were they on Synth?" Ratner asked as they had disappeared. "Are you?"

Darren laughed out loud. "That's the thing, right? You can't tell! We might all be tripping balls and you would never be able to figure it out. I might be on planet Bazoonga right now, but you will still think I'm here with you. That's why the ruling powers of this city are so frightened by Synth, man. The next revolution will be invisible—and unstoppable."

Ratner nodded politely. "Sure. But one last thing: where do you buy Synth if there aren't any dealers, like you said? How would I find some?"

Darren crossed his arms over his small chest. "You've got to be connected, man. That's the only way. And I'm sorry, but I've got a lot of work to do. Music doesn't produce itself, you know."

Ratner stood up and shook hands with the record producer. "Thanks for answering my questions. I highly appreciate it."

"No problem. It was actually interesting to meet a cop who knew something about music."

Never thought my wild youth would help me in my cop job, the city commissioner thought as he walked down the concrete stairs.

4

On the ride back to his office, Ratner asked the officer who was driving to turn on the radio. He tried to find a channel playing DAO, but gave up. Still not totally mainstream, as he had told Darren. Sometimes he regretted being right.

The commissioner's thoughts drifted to Jesse Valentino and his incredibly beautiful, melancholy blue eyes. Ratner had often tortured his younger colleague with industrial jazz playing full blast as they drove to some crime scene or another. The memory made him smile, and he shifted his position in his seat.

Music had always been an important element in Ratner's life. Like art, it offered so many possibilities of interpretations which contrasted drastically with his job—one murder, one explanation. Period. Music was a welcome uncertainty, a freedom of choices, an endless universe of stories.

He wondered what music Valentino actually listened to. He couldn't remember if he had ever asked him about it. He regretted it now. There were so many things he ignored about his ex-colleague. And now it was too late to ask him, unless one believed in ghosts and necromancy. The only thing he could do now is find out who had murdered him, and why.

Death was a two-sided door, which simultaneously could be shut and open. The trick was not to step through it, but it lay, invisible, at the end of a pitch black corridor we called "life" and when you mistakenly pushed it, it was too late. For you and those who loved you—all dumbstruck, all powerless and sometimes, secretly, all relieved.

5

Jesse Valentino's ghost followed him all day, a shimmering silvery silhouette Ratner could perceive standing in a dark corner of his consciousness. It wasn't threatening or even frightening, just there, silent, motionless, perhaps waiting, perhaps only a residual image like the one left by the sun on your eye when you walked from a sunny street into a place filled with shadow.

Walking into his empty apartment, Ratner noticed a note on the fridge. Laura had written that he shouldn't wait for her for dinner because she had a union meeting. Sighing, he opened the fridge and stared at the blank emptiness staring back at him. He took out his phone and dialed the Chinese takeaway. He almost ordered a dish for Valentino, but he remembered that ghosts didn't eat. So he asked for two bottles of Tsingtao beers. At least they could toast instead.

6

Ratner ate his dinner watching the news channel, to keep in touch with the general apocalyptic atmosphere. He saw Rust, Delgado, a few wars, some ecological disasters and a new superhero film trailer. Ads in between, like pop art collages. Valentino's ghost sat next to him, his blue eyes shining like a weak electrical flame. Valentino's Tsingtao bottle stood untouched on the table, so Ratner grabbed it and took a swig.

"I hope you don't mind, Captain," he told the ghost, "but all these horrors made me thirsty."

The ghost said nothing and didn't move. It just remained where it was, like a beautiful and useless piece of avant-garde furniture.

Ratner stood up, shaking his right leg which had fallen asleep.

"Okay, I think you're trying to tell me something," he said to the ghost. "And I think I know what it is."

He walked to his room and picked up his laptop, which he brought back and put down on the table, next to the remnants of his dinner.

"I am going to order your last collection, so we can both have a peaceful conscience."

Ratner googled "Jesse Valentino poet," quickly found the page of his publisher and clicked on the link. A fine cover appeared, with a nice illustration. It was titled *Verses from the Dark Side*.

Good title, Ratner thought. He had never heard of the publisher which had a really strange name—Two Hands Two Feet Press—but then again, that wasn't really surprising considering Ratner's lack of contemporary culture. He tried to find a link to order it, but to no avail. You apparently had to go to the publisher to buy the collection, or find a bookseller that carried it. He remembered his last visit to the bookstore and thought that going straight to the publisher would be his best bet. He typed the address on his phone. He would go as soon as he found some time.

"At least I tried," he said to the ghost.

The ghost answered nothing.

7

Ratner was already in bed reading when Laura came back—a history book about the emergence of the first city-states around 6000 BC. The author argued that the creation of the first large urban centers were the end of direct democracy and led to the creation of centralized and authoritarian governments.

"We're going to strike," Laura said as she began undressing. "Actually, it's going to be a general strike. The trade unions will announce it tomorrow. Fuck the power."

Ratner nodded noncommitted, his finger stuck between the pages of the thick volume. He wondered if they fucked the power too in Ur, Akkad and Sumer.

XIV. TEMPERANCE

Temperance: Missing the hippie sixties. Pouring yourself a glass of wine while sleepwalking. The possibility of flying. A TV ad for bleach. Remembering you have a heart. Having to choose between a holiday in the countryside or taking a hike in the mountains. Considering meeting an angel as an objective coincidence.

1

The general strike announcement was all over the morning media. As if it wasn't bad news enough, the unions called for a huge demonstration the following Saturday. The city commissioner shut the morning paper Mrs. Gardiner left every day on his desk and grabbed his cup of coffee. The office phone rang and he picked it up. It was DA Flowers. Of course.

"Georg! Did you see the news?"

"Yes."

"That is bad news. Really bad news. I need you in my office right now. Mayor Tchebick is already here."

"Sure. I'll be right over."

Ratner put down his mug next to the paper. When he would return, the news would be old and the coffee cold. *I'm a poet*, he thought, *and I didn't even know it.*

2

"Sit down, Ratner."

Mayor Tchebick was as polite as ever. *Good to see some things never change,* the commissioner thought as he grabbed the vacant seat in front of the DA's immaculate desk. The commissioner glanced around the room as he sat down. Tchebick sat next to him, dwarfing the desk and everybody around it with his huge presence. DA Flowers sat across from them, looking tense and uneasy. There was a fourth person sitting on the other side of Tchebick, a man in a petroleum-colored jacket with thinning dyed blond hair and thick Bordeaux-colored rimmed glasses.

"City Commissioner Georg Ratner, Josh Bing. Josh is head of President Delgado's strategic team for the campaign."

The two men briefly nodded to each other.

"We have also invited Sharon Stiegler, of the Workers' United Force union, but she declined," Flowers informed him.

"That's very regrettable," Bing said in a surprisingly soft voice. "It would have been good to hear her reasons to call for a general strike this weekend."

Haven't you guys read the papers or watched TV the past six months? Georg thought. *Jesus.*

"Yeah, bad timing. Really fucking bad timing," Tchebick grunted. "Now Rust is going to go ballistic on us about social issues."

"The reason we're all here, is to discuss the way we need to handle that demonstration on Saturday," Flowers said. "I think it's important we are in agreement on this."

"Clubber the ungrateful assholes," Tchebick said. "Send them crying home and make them appreciate we still have free hospitals running in this goddamn city."

"Now, now, Mayor," Bing objected."We know how you feel about this and we agree that the citizens might not have completely understood yet that the measures President Delgado has undertaken might seem drastic, but are in fact, necessary. But I am not sure antagonizing the people now would help us much for the campaign."

"People have become too comfortable," Tchebick grunted. "Back in my days..."

What? Ratner thought. *You would have shot them?*

"Well, Mayor, democracy wasn't then what it is today, if I may say," Bing interrupted.

"Gentlemen," Flowers chirped in, diplomatically. "We know that President Delgado has set up this meeting so that we could agree on a common position. Maybe we should ask the city commissioner what he thinks about the situation."

Ratner reclined on his chair, crossing his arms on his chest.

"Listen, all I know is that my position is to be in the line of fire. I am willing to take some political bullets, because that's my job. But I think my opinion doesn't really matter here. I think Mr. Bing here is the decision maker. He has probably already discussed the situation with President Delgado last night or early this morning. I may be old, but I'm not naive. So, Mr. Bing, how should I tell my forces to behave?"

Bing looked at the city commissioner with eyes that betrayed both irritation and concession. Tchebick shrugged, growling something unintelligible.

"Very well," Bing sighed, like an uncovered spy in a bad play. "It is clear that President Delgado doesn't want fuel poured onto the fire—and any violence coming from the police force would be used by our opponents to their advantage.

"However, if we do nothing, we will be considered weak. So, what I was going to suggest was this: a massive police presence—but with definite and clear orders of restraint."

Ratner thought about the possibility of Laura demonstrating Saturday. He would really insist on the "restraint" part.

"Sounds good to me," Ratner nodded. "I can go with that."

"Excellent!" Flowers said, obviously relieved. "I will set the details down with the city commissioner and the various District Commissioners as soon as we have the exact plan and schedule of the demonstration."

Tchebick stood up, cast a venomous glance on the three others and shrugged. "Fucking middle-class whiners," he grumbled. "I would have kicked their asses to the moon. One-way trip. Forever."

3

Ratner was sitting behind his desk, lost in his thoughts and playing the same four notes on an invisible piano when Mrs. Gardiner walked in, carrying a thick collection of files under her right arm. She dropped the bundle like a heavy bomb in front of him and was about to turn around when he stopped her.

"Do you have a minute, Mrs. Gardiner? Would you sit down and have a coffee with me? It just occurred to me that we have never really chatted together."

She smiled.

"Of course. I'll get us a cup."

She came back a few minutes later and sat down in front of him. Ratner realized then he didn't really know what he wanted from her.

"So . . ." he started, "I would like to know if you're happy here, with your work and all."

"Yes, very. I mean, I really liked City Commissioner Klein—Gus, as he wanted me to call him—but I only worked for him the past two years and he was already sick, so there were good days and not-so-good days, if you know what I mean. With you, it's been really smooth so far. What's more, I feel you give me more responsibilities, and I really appreciate that."

That's because I'm new on the job and I don't know anything about anything, Ratner thought. "Well, ahem, of course. You are so efficient, why wouldn't I trust you?"

Mrs. Gardiner's smile grew radiant.

"Can I ask you a personal question? I mean, not personal personal, but I would like your honest opinion."

"Sure."

"You heard about the general strike next Monday and the demonstration this Saturday, right? What do you think of that? I mean, is the situation in the city that bad?"

Mrs. Gardiner put down her cup and crossed her arms on her chest. "Well, I'll put it this way, Commissioner: it's been tough times for a lot of people here, including your men in the force. It's time the higher-ups realize that."

Ratner scratched his head. "What do you think I should do?"

"Call the union rep. Talk with him. That would be a step in the right direction."

Ratner nodded pensively. "Yes, of course. Of course. Thanks for the advice."

Mrs. Gardiner stood up and collected his empty cup of coffee. "Thank you for the chat, Commissioner."

"Call me Georg. I hope we will be working more than two years together."

"Call me Emma."

He smiled to her as she shut the door. He looked for his cigarettes and, grunting, picked up the phone to call the union rep.

4

Putting the phone down, the city commissioner felt relieved. The union representative was an intelligent and articulate woman, and the thirty minutes of conversation had been very civilized. Ratner had actually agreed with Donna—that was her name—about the general situation and what should be done about it. Donna had also said that she understood the city commissioner's difficult position, and that she was glad that they had spoken. The lines hadn't moved, and Ratner knew that he was heading for a storm of yet unknown magnitude, but at least he didn't feel like the totally hated captain of the ship. That would always be a consolation if he ever ended marooned on some desert island.

5

He buzzed Mrs. Gardiner and she walked in again, her reading glasses in her hand.

"Yes?"

"I just wanted to thank you for your suggestion that I call the union rep. We just spoke on the phone. It was a good talk."

The secretary smiled and he thought he saw some sparkles in her eyes.

"That was just an idea . . . Georg."

Ratner smiled in his turn. "Well, it was a good idea, Emma."

She waved her fingers as she shut the door behind her, and Georg looked for his cigarettes, wondering if Emma was a union member. He would have to ask her one of these days. And maybe join the union himself. Donna sounded like a good, efficient and rational person.

He also decided he would try and find Valentino's book later in the afternoon. Some poetry would be welcome to alleviate the dark and heavy complexities of the times.

6

The place had been torched. One could still read the words on the blackened sign, *Two Hands Two Feet Press*. According to the officers on the scene, a body lay in the basement and the stairs down were blocked by debris. There was a police line across the charred door. The rest of the five story building was relatively intact, save for the blackened façade.

Ratner sighed with discouragement. He felt like smoking.

The communion of places.

He searched in the pockets of his coat and stuck a cigarette between his chafed lips. There went his last chance to buy Valentino's poetry collection. It felt like a curse had befallen on his poor ex-colleague. First murdered, then all his books wiped out. He would check up on that fire.

He thought about the Samarqandi cop who had contacted him—Bassam, or whatever his name was. Hadn't the man told Ratner to contact him if the publisher was attacked too? Probably just a dead-end conspiracy theory, but Ratner felt obliged to explore all the possibilities.

He walked back to the car that was waiting for him, feeling depressed and angry. The only thing that warmed him up a little bit was the cigarette. It was a very thin and slightly bitter consolation.

7

Back in his office, Ratner called the fire department headquarters. He was told the investigation was still going on, but everything pointed to arson. A glass projectile, probably a bottle containing a flammable solution, had been thrown into the place. The publisher, a certain Lynn French, had unfortunately died in the fire.

Ratner thanked the officer, hung up and took out his personal phone. He calculated it would be about one a.m. in Samarqand but everybody knew cops didn't sleep. He swiped the Skype phone call button.

8

"Inspector General Shakr Bassam speaking. Who is this?"

Bassam's voice sounded tired and Georg suddenly felt bad about calling him so late.

"Georg Ratner, from New Babylon."

The voice cleared suddenly. "Ah, Georg! Lovely to hear from you! Anything new on Valentino's case?"

"As a matter of fact, yes." Ratner hesitated. "His publisher was a victim of arson. She is dead."

There was a long silence on the other end of the line. "Hmm . . . as I feared," Bassam finally mumbled. "We cannot jump to conclusions, but it does smell funny, as they say in your country."

"Yes, it does," Ratner agreed, although he had never heard that expression before. "And I'm very sad I cannot get his book now."

"Well, that can be arranged," Bassam said.

"What do you mean?" Ratner asked.

"I know who has copies. At least two. That's the way we always do it. You have to go to the magic mountain. You will find the book there."

Ratner suddenly realized he must be speaking to some mystic lunatic and regretted his call. "The magic mountain," he repeated automatically, as if it would make more sense.

"Yes, it's a bookstore.The name comes from the German novelist Thomas Mann. Very appropriate, I think. They will have it there. And Doug Hale, the owner, will explain all about the Egregorians and what we do. And he will have the book. I know this because he is the one who contacted me about Valentino's murder."

"Ah, a bookstore," Ratner said, relieved. "I don't think I ever heard of it."

"It's very small—on purpose," Bassam explained. "Doug will be happy to meet you."

"Thank you," Ratner said. "I will check it out."

"Thank you for calling me, Georg. And keep me posted. This could be very serious. The égrégore might be bigger and more advanced than we thought. Have a good day!"

9

Ratner was still thinking about his conversation with Shakr Bassam as he smoked a cigarette, looking at the city slowly disappearing in the winter's early evening fog. The last thing he needed was a self-appointed psychic messing with his investigation. Then again, he himself talked to an Egyptian goddess in his dreams, and her advice had actually helped him every time.

He walked back to his desk and killed his smoke in the ashtray. He looked at his watch and decided to go home. Enough nonsense for today. He would have a completely rational evening watching something on TV and drinking a nice whisky with ice cubes and a splash of water. Rational, normal and under control. Like his life should always be.

XV. THE DEVIL

The Devil: Having a bad hangover day. Feeling like smoking. Fear of getting fat and hairy. Chicken burning in the oven. Two perverse friends trying to make nice. Listening to the television for oracles. Waiting for a nice and powerful storm to clean the atmosphere.

1

Commissioner Dany Lacroix shut the door behind Ratner as he stepped into Lacroix's office. The place was still impeccably well kept, except for a pile of printed papers crowding the Financial Department cop's desk. Ratner glanced at the spreadsheets as he sat down, which were scribbled with red felt pen and underlined in yellow and green. The muscular man sat down in his turn and grabbed one of the sheets, turning it so Ratner could read it.

"I think Captain Valentino might have been onto something big—bigger than him and even bigger than us, perhaps."

Ratner looked at the columns, figures and scribbles, trying to make some sense out of them. "Oh," he said politely, waiting for Lacroix to continue.

"I actually had my office checked for bugs before calling you," the man said, in a lower voice.

"That big, hey?" Ratner tentatively joked.

Lacroix nodded, not joking. "I can't be really sure yet, but if my feeling is right, it could be huge. Well, as you can see, these are financial operations. Buying coffee for the Green Star company. Various companies, various places. All legit, but . . ."

Ratner waited for the second shoe to fall.

"Green Star isn't the one doing the buying."

Ratner squinted at the sheet. "It says Green Star here."

Lacroix nodded with a wry smile. "Yes, it does. But we checked on Green Star. It's actually part of larger holding. It's financed by a fund called S & G."

"S & G? Never heard of it."

"Precisely. Very, very discreet. Offshore and considered more than shady. Suspected of laundering money for the big cartels, among other things, which include illegal weapon sales through the Dark Net. And guess who is their legal representative here?"

"Gonzalez?"

"Bingo."

Ratner scratched his head. "I still don't see what's so suspicious here. Many companies are owned by funds. How much of Green Star is owned by S & G?"

"Sixty per cent. 59.9 to be exact."

"Which means Sam Rosen is the minority owner of its own company?"

"Yessir."

"Hmm."

"Hmm, indeed."

"So you think Green Star might be a front for some other kind of operation, right? Is that just a gut feeling or is there more?"

Lacroix sat back on his chair, looking serious. "Harding died, Valentino died and they are both connected to Green Star, directly or indirectly."

"True," Ratner agreed.

"We don't know how much Harding or Valentino knew about the S & G connection, but we can assume that Harding had seen some papers, or whatever. The connection is not obvious and it took quite a lot of research for my people to find that out."

"Hidden is always suspicious," Ratner commented.

"Indeed," Lacroix agreed. "But the whole situation gets more complicated . . . I mean waaay more complicated . . . I have to show you something."

Lacroix opened his laptop and searched for a file. A picture appeared of President Delgado standing next to a handsome man with a Robert Redford haircut. Both were smiling and shaking hands.

"It's Sam Rosen next to the president," Lacroix said, explaining the obvious. "This picture was taken last month during a fund-raising rally."

"Damn," Ratner said.

"But wait, that's not all," Lacroix gloated nervously. "It gets even better. One of the heavy guys in S & G is Ted Rust, through another offshore company, Sunshine Mountain. His son-in-law is the CEO of Sunshine Mountain."

Ratner sighed and rubbed his chin. "Hence the Gonzalez connection. She works for Rust, Green Star and S & G. And probably Sunshine Mountain too." he said.

"Yes, she does. And that's why I thought it wise to call you before we carried on our investigation," Lacroix said. "It might get political if we find anything."

Ratner suddenly felt like the spreadsheets had morphed into an ominous time bomb. "How many people have you involved?"

"Four. Only my closest colleagues."

Ratner's mind shifted into fifth gear with a rattling sound. "Good. We have to maintain a very low profile, but let's see where this takes us. Focus on S & G and their history with Sam Rosen and Ted Rust. Check out the companies they're buying coffee from, and make sure that this coffee really exists, or that it is indeed coffee they're buying. If you run into any kind of trouble or obstruction attempt, let me know. If you need any warrants, come to me directly. And keep me posted, of course."

"You bet."

Ratner stood up and turned around before leaving. "You know that this could either earn you a big promotion or end your career, right?"

Lacroix shrugged, still sitting behind his desk. "I appreciated Captain Valentino," he said. "He was a good cop."

"And an excellent poet," Ratner said, as he opened the door.

And an excellent poet, he repeated to himself as he walked toward the elevator, finding the words, strangely, both sad and comforting.

3

For the first time since he had accepted his new position, Ratner asked Mrs. Gardiner if she would like to have lunch with him at the cafeteria. She accepted and they found themselves chatting in front of an egg and bacon sandwich for him, and a vegetable quiche for her. They laughed a lot, and Ratner felt good as he sat back down behind his desk. Human warmth was hard to find these days, and it was a precious thing one should always cherish. He promised himself to remember that and to buy some flowers for Laura on the way home.

4

"City Commissioner Ratner speaking."

"Hi Commissioner, this is Eris Jordan. I wanted to let you know we've got some info concerning Darren Deich."

Ratner had Deich under surveillance since his visit to the producer at his studio, because he actually was the only real lead they had. Someone who produced music directly inspired by an illegal drug had to have connections. You didn't need a PhD to know that.

"Yes? I'm listening."

"He's organizing a small DAO festival by the harbor next Sunday evening. Also a political event, it seems: all the money raised will go to the unions. The whole team will be there, plus a few extras."

"Excellent. I'll be there too, in the HQ van. Did he ask for an official authorization?"

"Not as far as I know. But I'll check."

"Yes, please do that. It can give us a good excuse to jump in and make a few arrests. Tchebick and Flowers would like that, I think."

"For sure," Jordan said and he felt her ironic smile. "They would even give you a hug."

They laughed and she hung up.

With that general strike coming up, Delgado would appreciate any positive bit coming from the police, even if it was only symbolic. Or rather, *especially* if it was symbolic.

5

Laura was on the phone discussing plans for the upcoming demonstration, when Ratner walked into their apartment. He turned the news channel on and watched some experts discuss the impact of the strike on Delgado's chances to be re-elected. Laura shut her phone and sat next to him.

"You're home late," she said.

"I was actually at a meeting about the demonstration tomorrow," he answered, suddenly feeling very tired.

"Did you discuss if you were going to clubber us and teargas us or not?" Laura asked, half-malicious, half-provoking.

"Something like that," he answered.

It had been a long strategic reunion, which had lasted over three hours. The whole brass was there. People had been sweating, arguing and, well, Tchebick mostly, cursing. Bing had been present too, of course, and said he held Ratner responsible for a peaceful ending to the demonstration. Flowers had backed Ratner up, saying he had "complete trust in this man." A perfect epitaph.

"Just be careful out there," Ratner added, looking at Laura directly in the eye. "You never know what can happen."

"Are you warning me about something or just patronizing me?" Laura asked, moving away from him.

Ratner smiled. "No, no—neither. I just care about you, that's all. And I can only control so much regarding the situation tomorrow. It's basically out of my hands now, although I am officially in charge. You know how it is."

"No, I don't, actually, but I can imagine. And yes, I will be careful. I will not throw stones at the police or smash bank windows. I will just walk down Lermontov Avenue with my colleagues and about half-a-million other pissed-off people."

"Don't get hurt," Ratner said, putting his arm around her shoulders. "That's what matters to me."

And don't get arrested, he added for himself. He could imagine Tchebick's ire and Rust's glee should the city commissioner's very own wife be locked up with her fellow demonstrators. Laura cuddled up against him and her warmth relaxed him. He kissed her hair and suddenly realized he had forgotten to buy her flowers. *Love* sometimes was indeed just a word.

XVI. THE TOWER

The Tower: Fear of heights. Premature ejaculation. Following an arrow. Dreaming of skyscrapers. Planning a visit to New York. Joining a conspiracy to bring down the king. Unexpected fireworks. Getting rid of noisy neighbors.

1

Ratner watched the demonstration unfurl on Lermontov Avenue on the multiple video screens set up in the HQ van. It was a massive living entity, slow and colorful. It was also powerful, although its strength was still unknown. It could become violent at any moment and show its claws and spit out flames like a wounded dragon, or remain peaceful like a huge alligator taking a tranquil stroll along a golf course.

The weather was nice, considering it was December—a blue sky and a beautiful sun, although the temperature was just a little over freezing point. Ratner watched the images sent by the helicopters hovering over the beast like powerless flies. He tried to find Laura's face for a little while, but gave up. To see her would have stressed him more than necessary.

The city commissioner listened closely to the orders, comments and questions exchanged between the various police entities—the plain clothes, the riot units, the uniformed officers. Although it was cold in the van, he had taken off his coat and was sweating. His eyes stung with the salty drops that once in a while rolled down his forehead. On the other side of the van, right behind him, Flowers and Bing were watching the live reports on the news channels, and discussing them.

Ratner thought about Mayor Tchebick and President Delgado, probably sitting together in the presidential house and waiting nervously for the day to end. He wondered if they were biting their nails or just watched the whole thing with royal distance and disdain. Power and distance did walk hand in hand. And distance was how you could judge the value of your own power: Ratner, for instance, had no power at all. He was in the dead middle of it all, in the heart of the hurricane's screaming whirlwind.

2

"Camera Seventeen, can you focus on the corner of Lermontov Avenue and Puchkin Street?"

"Camera Two, zoom in on that group of people next to the red Subaru van."

"Yes, officer Smith, let the people march toward the Museum of Modern Art, but not toward Armstrong park. I repeat, not toward Armstrong park."

"Camera Thirty-seven, your image is blurry."

"Yes, Smith, you may use tear gas if a group tries to move toward the park. But only after you have warned them. Keep me posted."

"Camera Thirty-seven, your image is still blurry."

"Camera Two, can you follow the group for a little while. Yes, the five people with the backpacks."

"Camera Fourteen, keep tracking the group under that *The Revolution Will Be Invisible And Absolute* banner."

"Camera Thirty-seven, the image is fine now, thank you."

3

To everyone's relief, the demonstration disbanded quietly around six p.m., in the cold half-darkness of the late afternoon. Some small groups of Black Bloc–inspired youths tried to attack the police and managed to smash some shop windows and burn a few cars, but that happened near the end of the demonstration and the troublemakers were rapidly arrested. Of course, the media focused on these incidents, but that was also predictable. How could sharks survive without the scent of blood?

Sitting in the car driving him back to the police department building for a debriefing, Ratner massaged his eyes and reclined in his seat. It had, however, been a huge demonstration indeed, a monster of more than half-a-million protesters, of all ages, backgrounds and incomes.

He wondered if Delgado had got the message, or if she would carry on with her "bitch, please" attitude, which had cost her so many future votes in the past months. His bet was on the latter: politicians lived in a world apart, where they knew better than anybody else, because their vision was how the world really was—and anything not fitting into that vision simply didn't exist.

Ratner didn't think it was intentionally evil or even narcissistic, but that was just how power transformed a person's sense of reality. In that way, power was a drug much more dangerous than Synth, but also much more difficult to fight against. Who would declare power illegal, except for the dreamy anarchist? He immediately thought of Laura and grunted.

"Yes. Commissioner?" said his driver, a young woman with short black hair.

"Oh, nothing, Sergeant. Just thinking about anarchists. And how right they might be once in a while."

"Anarchists, sir?"

"Never mind. Just drive."

4

Rust was all over the news and Delgado nowhere to be seen. The media claimed the demonstration had been a great success for the unions and a wake-up call to the president—if she deigned to hear it.

Ratner brought the glass of whisky to his lips, enjoying the rich flavors the water and the ice brought out. He looked at his watch, wondering what Laura was doing. It was past nine in the evening now, and the demonstration had been over for hours. He had tried to call her a couple of times, but she hadn't answered. His logical mind told him that she was fine, probably celebrating their "victory" or "success" with friends and colleagues, but his irrational self worried about her getting arrested, or worse. Knowing her, Laura would probably have hidden her identity and her connection to him as long as possible, just to make things more difficult for everybody.

Of course, he could have just called Flowers and asked him if he had any info about her being in custody instead of worrying in front of the TV, but it would have also been too simple. He and Laura enjoyed life with a certain degree of complexity. *And trust*, he quickly added for himself. *Yes, trust.* But he glanced at his watch one more time anyway.

5

He was about to finally give Flowers a call when he heard the key turn in the lock of their front door.

"Sorry I'm so late," Laura said, taking her coat off. "I was at a post-demonstration debriefing."

"That's what I thought," Ratner lied, putting his phone back in his pocket.

"Well," she said, sitting down next to him. "Won't you congratulate me?" Her breath smelled of food and alcohol.

"Congratulate you for what?"

"For our big success today. Half a million in the streets. Yay!"

"Delgado losing three points in the polls, yay!" Ratner retorted, slightly irritated.

He knew his irritation came more from worrying about Laura's whereabouts than the political outcome of the demonstration, but he couldn't tell her that. She would have laughed and told him he shouldn't patronize her.

"Well, I hope she will react now. The ball's in her camp."

"The ball is mainly in Rust's camp," he snapped.

"Whose fault, Georg? Whose fault?"

Ratner shrugged and stood up to pour himself another whisky. It was a Sunday tomorrow, so a little hangover didn't matter.

"Pour me one too," Laura said.

He heard his name as he walked back into the sitting room. Laura put a finger to her lips and increased the volume on the TV. It was Rust.

"City Commissioner Ratner is a coward and a soft-hearted humanist. He should have acted much more strongly about this leftist provocation. Much, much more strongly!"

"And we need much more grammarly grammar," Laura sighed as Ratner sat next to her.

She ran her hand through his graying hair. "My poor baby," she whispered. "Attacked by a moron on live TV."

Ratner grunted. "If he ever becomes president, I'll blame it on you forever."

"I can live with the guilt," Laura said, chugging down her drink.

She looked at him and laughed, and Ratner knew he could live with the guilt too.

XVII. THE STAR

The Star: Watering the garden at night. Dreaming of becoming an astronaut. Being blinded by a camera flash. Searching for inspiration in the sky. The beauty of night. Finding the right one at a hippie festival. Counting your blessings.

1

Ratner had forgotten he had to work this Sunday and his hangover nagged him slightly. He had drunk the rest of the whisky bottle with Laura last night, discussing politics and the future of New Babylon. She had called him a "conservative" and he had called her a "utopian," which were actually terms of endearment in their relationship. Laura had finally asked him if they should get a cat, and he had still said no although he was very drunk, which for him proved that his meaning was definite. She had gone to bed miffed and he had fallen asleep sitting on the sofa.

And now, here he was, sitting in an unmarked police van, watching the video feeds being transmitted by plainclothes officers scattered around the DAO free festival. They were all wearing special glasses with nanovideo cameras mounted in the frames and spoke through nanomics hidden in their clothes. It was all very nano and terribly efficient.

The music from the festival blasted through the van's thin walls, which didn't help his hangover. Captain Eris Jordan was with him, giving orders and relaying Ratner's comments and advice to her team through her headset and microphone.

"Try to focus on that group around that Rasta guy, there," said Ratner.

Captain Jordan spoke into her mic, "Zoom in on the girl with the red parka. Yes, that one, with the paper bag. Is she selling anything? Can you check? You sure? Okay. Move on."

"I see Darren Deich. Get closer to him and don't let him out of your sight," said Ratner.

"I want a triangular surveillance system around Deich. Dean, Tammy and Wang, you guys are on. Keep rotating and keep him in sight."

Ratner continued to scrutinize the screen. Deich was walking through the crowd toward the scene, wearing a thick coat, and stopping once in a while to shake hands and small talk. He suddenly looked around and took a sharp turn left, toward one of the alleys leading to the parking lot."

"Be careful now," he said to the cop shadowing Deich. "Don't get noticed but get as close as you can."

He told Captain Jordan to send discreet backup to the parking lot.

A silhouette waited for Deich in the parking lot's half-darkness. A woman.

"Begin filming now," Ratner told the cop. "And film as long as you can."

The woman took a small backpack from her shoulder and opened it. She dug in and brought back a small bag of pills.

"Now," Ratner said. "Grab them."

"Police!" the cop shouted, and his hand appeared on the video, showing his badge. "Stop!"

"OK, everybody," Ratner cried out, "we're on! I repeat, we're on! Shut down the festival and arrest all the people you can!"

He turned to Captain Jordan, who was standing behind him.

"You can let the media in now."

On the screen, he saw Deich being arrested and the woman run away, uniformed cops after her. There were no images anymore, all the cops caught in the chaos on the ground.

"Eris, what's the channel to the cops chasing that girl?"

"377, I think. Or 388."

Ratner grabbed the microphone and tried both frequencies.

"388," a voice answered, panting.

"This is 01, 388. What is your situation? Over."

"The girl is gone, Chief. Can't find her anywhere. It's like she vanished into thin air. Over."

"Keep looking, 388. She can't be far. Over."

At least we've got Deich, and we shut down an illegal Synth-inspired music festival, the commissioner thought, waiting for 388 to come back on air with some good news. *Tchebick is going to like that. Tchebick is going to like that very, very much.*

2

Mayor Tchebick did like that very much indeed and called for a press conference later that same evening, asking Ratner to be present to say a few words about the operation. The media unanimously talked about a "major crackdown operation" and Rust tweeted that it was just a PR stunt set up to give DAO music a wider audience. Ratner thought it was a very minor and dubious half-failed operation as they didn't catch the girl, but smiled nonetheless to the cameras while shaking victorious hands with Tchebick and Flowers.

3

Most of the people who were arrested at the DAO concert were freed the following day, but Deich remained locked up and charged with possession of illegal substances. Twelve pellets of Synth were found on him, enough to threaten him with an additional "intention to sell" charge which could send him to jail for ten years, instead of the usual six months. And that was without considering "organization of an illegal event on public property."

When Ratner walked into the interrogation cell, he found Deich slumped over the table, looking down at his manacled hands. His lawyer sat next to him, a bearded hipster in his mid-thirties with probably a very limited experience of the realities of criminal law, if any at all. Ratner was accompanied by Captain Eris Morgan and another officer from the drug squad, who had the task to record the interview on video.

Captain Jordan proceeded with all the legal announcements and presentations, enumerating the charges and naming all the people present in the room.

Ratner and Jordan shook hands with the lawyer, then sat down.

"Sorry to see you in trouble, Warren," Ratner said, "But you put yourself in pretty deep shit here. I mean, I know people did that in the sixties, organizing free concerts and giving free drugs and all, but this is now. And Synth isn't popular enough to protect you. Not yet, maybe later, but not now for sure."

"We weren't giving out free drugs," Warren answered, now looking defiantly at the commissioner through his glasses.

He might have been a small man, but he didn't lack courage, Ratner thought.

"We organized this concert to support the unions."

"Yeah, and are the unions supporting you now?" Ratner asked. "Are they paying for your lawyer?"

Deich and his lawyer exchanged a quick glance, and the music producer shrugged, shaking his head.

"See? You're all alone here. All alone with us. And you know what we have on you. It can cost you up to ten years, easy."

"It was for my personal use," Deich protested.

"How can you prove that?" Jordan snapped.

"Well, I . . ."

"You don't have to answer that," Deich's lawyer interjected. "We're not at the trial yet. They have to prove you had an intention to sell first. And that will be very difficult."

Ratner was a little impressed. The guy did know his stuff after all.

"True," the commissioner admitted, "but right now, Synth is considered a major threat in this city. So the judges will be tougher. It might not be fair, I agree, but that's the way it's going to be. So you have a choice, Warren: you collaborate with us, or we bring the entire house down on your shoulders."

Deich's eyelids flicked. "Collaborate? In what way?"

Ratner reclined in his chair. "Tell us what you know. Everything you know about Synth and how it's distributed in this city. Give us names. Who this girl is, for instance. The one who sold you the drugs."

"I'm not a snitch," Deich said.

A classic, Ratner thought, remaining silent.

"And what do I get in the bargain?" Deich resumed, exchanging a glance with his lawyer, who gave him a short nod.

"Well, you have very serious charges hanging over your head," Ratner said, looking at Jordan for support. "And possession is the least serious. So, we could drop the intention of selling, and minimize the illegal concert event—like giving you a ticket, for example."

"Don't get impressed, Warren," the lawyer said. "Like I just told you, they have to *prove* the intention of selling, which is impossible. The other two charges are nothing."

"Possession is still up to two years," Jordan said.

"Yep," Ratner agreed. "And whatever your lawyer says, it's still no fun to spend six months in a New Babylon cell."

Deich was thinking, biting the nail of his right thumb. He obviously didn't like the way things were going.

"Can I walk out of here free?" he asked.

"No, but we can ask a judge to reduce your sentence to three months and a fine. Two even, if we're lucky," Jordan explained.

Deich nodded. "I can't tell you much about this girl," he finally said. "But I know her name. Vita. And I think she's a foreigner. She has a slight accent."

Ratner wasn't surprised to hear the name. It was the same the other guy they had busted had given them. "Does she have other people working with her?"

Deich shook his head. "Not that I know of. I only dealt with her. And I know other people have too. It's like she's the only dealer in the whole town."

Ratner frowned. "There are twelve million people living in New Babylon. I don't believe that's possible, son."

"She's the only one who ever sold the drug to me. Or my friends. Although I won't give any names," Deich quickly added.

"Can you help us draw an identikit? That would help us a lot. And the judge would like that," Jordan said.

Deich nodded, and his lawyer tapped him on the shoulder. A friendly, relieved pat.

Walking out of the room, Ratner felt both happy and frustrated. They had something that Flowers, Tchebick and Delgado would be very glad for: a name and a face. But he also knew that it amounted, in reality, to almost nothing.

4

Back in his office he called Flowers, looking at the city being itself, that is to say: ugly and indifferent.

"Hi, Jim. We got a perp who can identify a dealer. Jordan is with him right now. They're doing an identikit."

"Tchebick and Bing are going to love this," he said. "When can we have the identikit?"

"Later this afternoon, probably."

"Super. We'll make sure to release it to all the media as soon as possible. We want to crack down on that ring, fast! Great job, Georg. I always said you were the one for the job."

"Thanks, Jim. It's good to know."

Fuck the media, Ratner thought as he hung up. *Fuck the media and the politicians they rode in on.*

5

Laura was already home fixing dinner when Ratner walked into their apartment. "Hmm, smells good," he said, taking off his coat. "What are you cooking?"

"Spaghetti Bolognese, the only dish I can manage not to burn. Or almost."

They kissed as she stirred the meat, tomato and parmigiano sauce.

"You are being unfair to yourself," Ratner said. "You can also make a good omelette."

She gave him a little slap on the chest and laughed. Laura was an excellent cook. No question about that. Her pasta dish did smell delicious. He, on the other hand, couldn't even make a simple omelette. Frozen pizza was the only thing he could cook. Or almost—for real.

"How come you're home so early?" he asked, as if suddenly waking up. "You usually come late on Tuesdays."

"The strike, remember? It's still going on."

Ratner nodded as if he knew, but he had actually forgotten everything about it. Too many things were happening at the same time.

The TV was on and Ratner grabbed himself a beer before sitting down on the couch. *Music producer busted for Synth possession* kept running in the breaking news ribbon at the bottom of the screen.

Ratner raised his beer in the air. "You're famous now, Warren Deich," he said out loud. "Congratulations!"

"What?" Laura asked from the kitchen.

"Nothing. I just helped someone get famous and promote his business today."

"Oh, that's so nice of you!" Laura said.

"Yes, indeed, it is," Ratner grunted. "He doesn't know it yet, but he will be thankful, one day."

It will be a mythical story, for sure, Ratner thought. *The birth of a new fucking rock 'n' roll legend. And all thanks to me.*

XVIII. THE MOON

The Moon: Seeing double. Yellow fever. Remembering you have to walk the dogs. Bad day at the seaside. Having to choose between two identical things. Memories of an eclipse. Looking for things in the sky.

1

The Magic Mountain Bookstore was located on a small side street off Greene Avenue. It wasn't difficult to find, but it was strangely discreet—a used books store with a few rare editions displayed in a dusty window, some signed, some not. Because of the strike and the lack of public transport, Ratner had asked his driver to drop him nearby. It wasn't very far from his apartment, so it wasn't a big detour, and it was easy for him to walk home.

Ratner tried the door. It was open and he walked in, slightly numbed from the cold winter evening. It was a small shop, with bookshelves running on all the walls. All the books were locked behind glass panels. The whole place smelled faintly of incense—a deep, nice smell.

A man stood up from behind a small counter wearing a classic British tweed suit, like the ones popular in the sixties, which contrasted with his shaggy longish gray hair and beard. It was impossible to give him an age—he could have been anywhere between his mid-forties to early seventies—and walking closer, Ratner noticed his beard had two thin braids on the sides.

"Welcome!" the man said. "What can I do for you?"

"Well, I was sent to your shop by a mutual . . . acquaintance, I think."

"Yes?"

The man stood motionless, a hand poised on his desk. His other hand rested on a straight ebony cane with a silver handle.

"Do you know someone from Samarqand, Ali Shakr Bassam?" Ratner cautiously asked.

The man smiled. "Yes, yes—of course. You must be Georg Ratner, the famous policeman! Sorry I didn't recognize you," he said with a friendly laugh. "Ali told me you would probably be coming. It's about Valentino, right?"

Ratner nodded and the man extended his hand. "Doug Hale. I'm the owner of the shop. Sorry for your loss. Ali told me you were close."

Ratner shook the hand somewhat mechanically. He wasn't used to be warmly welcomed in his job.

"I knew him too," Hale resumed. "He used to come here once in a while, and he participated in a couple of readings. We weren't close, but I was really shocked when I saw he had been murdered. Although, I must admit, not completely surprised."

"How do you mean?" Ratner asked, now genuinely interested.

"Well, you know, he was very political in his last collection. And not the way people like it these days. He had recently discovered the translated poetry of Olgeÿ Tazar and had become very interested in Samarqandi poetry. Not only that, but also Samarqandi religion. He told some of my friends he was even considering converting."

"Really?" Ratner was surprised. He had never considered his ex-colleague as a religious person. Or rather, the thought had never crossed his mind.

"He was supposedly working on a new collection inspired by Samarqand. Yes, our third most important enemy after New Moscow and New Beijing. You can imagine that some would be shocked by this, especially when an important poet like Valentino takes such a stance."

Ratner nodded. He could definitely imagine what would have happened with Valentino's job if he had converted. Maybe not fired—although that would have happened if Rust was elected, no doubt—but surely given some third zone desk duties.

"Did he post about this publicly?"

"Yes, he did. You can still see it on his site. The last two pieces—quite long, with two new poems. He got a lot of hateful comments, and threats too."

Ratner blamed himself for not having looked into this side of Valentino's life sooner. He now had three equal possibilities for a murder motive: the Green Star investigation, his political involvement or a stupid junkie that had seen his expensive watch.

"Ali told me you were an Egregorian, and that your role was to somehow fight bad vibes, if I understood correctly. So you're in politics too?" Ratner asked, genuinely curious now.

Hale, who had moved to one of the bookcases, turned around. "Well, yes, in a way. Ali explained what we do, right?"

Ratner nodded again. "Sort of. Our conversations were brief."

"I'm sure you think we're nuts," Hale said with a chuckle. "But, believe me, we're very serious."

He opened the glass front, took out a book and walked back to his desk.

"Come into my office," he said. "It'll be more comfortable to talk."

He opened a door which led to another room. Ratner followed him and was immediately struck by a poster of Nūt that decorated the opposite wall.

The back room was a cozy corner with three huge leather armchairs facing each other around a small round table. The walls were bare, save for the poster, but there was a beautiful Persian carpet on the floor. There were no windows, yet it didn't feel claustrophobic, perhaps because of the reassuring red warmth coming from the carpet. Another small table stood in a corner, holding a Chinese incense holder. A thin stick smoldered quietly, its thin perfumed smoke going straight up toward the ceiling.

"Nice," Ratner said, meaning it.

"Thank you," Hale said, showing him one of the armchairs with an open hand. "Please, take a seat."

Ratner looked at his watch, then remembered he had nothing better to do and relaxed. The armchair was very comfortable. Hale sat down in his turn, steadying himself with his cane. He handed Ratner the book he had picked from the shelves. It was Valentino's latest collection.

"How did you get that?" Ratner asked. "The press was torched basically on the day it was supposed to come out."

Hale's blue eyes darkened. "Yes, it's horrible. Poor Lynn, poor Jesse. The times are really hitting us hard."

"Do you think these murders are related?" Ratner asked, flipping through the book, feeling strangely moved by the object.

"Of course they are. We have studied the patterns. Rust, the economical situation in the city, the rise of racism and xenophobia. The égrégore is rising and is becoming harder to stop by the day. We really have to do something before it's too late."

"What do you do, exactly?" Ratner asked.

Hale caressed his beard thoughtfully. "We don't do anything directly, but we are an organization that has vowed to fight back against the evil monsters that sometimes arise around us, Commissioner. Ali may have told you, the Egregorian society was created in Istanbul, in 1934, at the time of the great Nazi auto-da-fés, the burning of books. You see, the attack on culture is always the first step for the creation of an égrégore, an uncontrollable monster created by a mass through its worst feelings and desires. Nazism was an égrégore, like Stalinism, and all the 'isms' and intolerant religious phenomena in the history of our poor world.

"Culture is the invisible structure of society, Commissioner, and the more diverse, the more beautiful it becomes. Égrégores, on the other hand, are the ultimate simplification, the reduction of complexity to something horribly simple."

"You mean a 'monster' killed Valentino and his publisher?"

"Not directly—an égrégore is immaterial—but it helped. It made it possible. No, not possible—it made it necessary, just as the murder of the Spanish poet Federico Garcia Lorca made the Franco dictatorship possible. And many others before and after him. And this is where we come in. We study the possibilities, evaluate the risks and begin the resistance. We are a passive organization, Commissioner, not an aggressive one. No worries here. But we organize countermeasures by collecting works, manuscripts, any kind of publication by writers or artists we feel are threatened by the égrégore. We store them in our vaults for later, so culture, in its multiplicity and openness, can finally triumph and prevail again."

"I see," Ratner said, half-lying. "But why have you contacted me? I mean, your organization?"

"To make you aware of what you are fighting against, Commissioner. It's not just criminals, it is a supernatural entity that wants to destroy everything that stands in its way."

Ratner nodded, his mind blank, staring straight at the Nūt poster. "One last question: why do you have this poster of Nūt?"

Hale smiled. "It's our symbol. She is the goddess of the night, invisible yet keeping everything together."

Ratner handed the book back to Hale, who shook his head.

"No, no. It's for you. We have several other copies, here in Babylon and in other cities. Valentino is safe with us. We will make sure he comes back in full daylight sometime in the future. Which we hope will be near."

"I hear you," Ratner said, standing up. "And thank you. It was a very interesting talk."

Walking out of the store, Ratner patted the pocket in which he had slipped Valentino's collection. The cold bit his nose and cheeks, but he didn't mind. The Egregorians might be a bunch of lunatics, but he was glad to have them on his side. He felt less lonely, and not as crazy as he usually thought he was.

2

At home, Ratner went online to Valentino's blog and checked the two entries Hale had mentioned.

The Egregorian had been right: Valentino did praise the Samarqandi faith and did indicate an intention to convert and support the Samarqandi cause. The comments were indeed full of insults and threats, from various individuals to organized groups.

He would call Captain Millborne, who was in charge of the investigation and ask her if she had seen this. The site could always open up for more possibilities. Of course, she would need more personnel, and given the cuts . . . Ratner mentally cursed Delgado and her stupid politics that didn't work. He could definitely understand the anger boiling around, although he couldn't understand the success of someone like Ted Rust, who incarnated all the reasons of the problem. Politics were definitely as irrational as faith, with the same dire consequences.

Speaking of irrational, Laura was sitting in front of him, playing with tarot cards. She had given him the deck a hundred years ago, telling him that it would help him focus on the problems in his life. He had never used the cards, but Laura did once in a while. And who was he to judge, having an Egyptian goddess as a secret adviser?

He stood up and walked behind her, softly massaging her shoulders.

"Hmm, that feels good," she said. "I'm getting all stiff not working. I miss those kids, you know?"

Ratner grunted, looking at the cards displayed in front of her. "What does it say? Good things or bad things?"

"Well, really good things, actually. You have The Sun, Judgment and The World. All cards of victory and success. Strange, given my question."

"Which was?"

"The way of the world. What is waiting ahead. Not exactly the feeling I get."

"For sure," Ratner said, digging his thumbs deep into Laura's shoulders. "You should do another reading."

Laura gathered the cards and put them back in their box. "Not tonight. I'd rather go to bed with the possibility of something good happening, for once."

Ratner nodded and kissed the top of her head. It smelled of shampoo and love. Well, mostly shampoo, and also conditioner. But love came in all sorts of smells, after all.

3

"Is this for real?" Laura asked, pressing the volume button up.

They were watching TV after dinner, and Delgado was making a surprise speech. It hadn't been announced, and she had just appeared on the eight o'clock evening news on all channels, talking from her office at the presidential palace.

"I think so," Ratner said.

"Did she just say we were 'in a state of social emergency and I hear you'? Oh my God, I'm dreaming!" Laura cried out.

"Wait for the rest, she hasn't finished yet," Ratner said, trying to remain calm although what he was hearing completely astounded him.

Delgado was making a complete U-turn on her political program. She said she had understood the protest and that she actually agreed with it. There should be more public jobs, more public spending, more control on banks and a better balance in taxes. It was a short speech, clearly delivered.

Laura turned to Ratner while frantic commentators began to discuss what everybody had just heard. "I just can't believe this," she said.

"The cards were right, it seems," Ratner said, smiling.

"That completely freaks me out, to be honest," Laura said.

"Are you going to vote for her now?"

Laura stood up and shrugged. "If she confirms it, absolutely. I think she will need all the votes she can muster after this."

On the screen Rust was accusing President Delgado of using cheap left-wing populism to score some desperately needed votes. Ratner had to admit he kind of agreed with the guy, but still hoped it would work. Hell, he might even vote for her too.

XIX. THE SUN

The Sun: Letting your kid do dangerous things. A nostalgia for summer. Waving the red flag like there is no tomorrow. Going to the horse races. Feeling like a holiday somewhere warm. Switching to sunflower oil in your cooking. Setting the controls for the heart of the sun.

1

Mrs. Gardiner let District Commissioner Lacroix in and Ratner rose from his chair to greet him.

"I'm sorry to barge on you like this, chief," Lacroix said as they shook hands. "But I thought it was important."

He was carrying a large box which seemed pretty heavy, and Ratner moved some stuff around on his encumbered desk to create some space.

Lacroix put the box down with a sigh, then opened it and began to take out thick binders with different names on them, five in all. He was sweating a little when he finished.

"We have focused on the companies Green Star is buying its coffee from. Five in all, all eco-friendly and fair-trade certified. Well, supposedly." Lacroix grinned.

"Supposedly?" Ratner asked, intrigued.

"Yes. My working hypothesis is that Harding knew that Sam Rosen and Green Star were just a front for something fishy and that Back To Earth sent him to investigate what exactly was going on. And this is what he found and gave to Valentino."

Lacroix opened one of the binders labeled *Blue Mist*.

"These are some of the spreadsheets that were on Valentino's USB key, right?"

Lacroix nodded. "Yes, but we went through all of them, analyzed them and gathered the intelligence in separate files—as you see now."

Ratner grunted, impressed. "A lot of work, I guess."

"I'll send you the overtime work hours forms to sign, don't worry. This allowed us to get a better picture of the whole system."

"I'm listening," Ratner said.

"You see, these five companies, Blue Mist, Future Sun, Equality First, Natural Nature and Holding Hands are all charities, linked to nonprofit organizations bearing the same name. But guess who is the largest donor? For all of them."

Ratner thought about it for a second. "I don't know," he admitted.

"S & G," Lacroix said triumphantly.

"Wow. You don't say," Ratner grunted. "That's something indeed. But tell me, why would S & G buy coffee from charities supported by themselves? Are they buying cheaper than the market? Is that the scam?"

Lacroix shook his head. "No, actually they're buying at a slightly higher price."

"I don't get it," Ratner began, then suddenly it struck him. "Unless . . . unless they're laundering money—laundering huge cash amounts as donations to charities, to reinvest the money in a clean business. Genius!"

"My thoughts exactly," Lacroix said. "And that's what we're investigating now. But I need your total support, because, given the situation, it could become a political powder barrel at some point."

"Yes, of course," Ratner said, nodding. "I can see that. I will cover you all the way, don't worry. You have my blessings. And try to see how much Rust knows about all this. If you can. But keep it secret for now and only work with colleagues you trust two hundred percent."

"No problem. Of course. I'll keep you closely in the loop."

When Lacroix was gone, Ratner looked at the empty space on the desk where the cardboard box had stood. It looked like the eye of a hurricane, and he wondered what it would destroy in its path.

2

Ratner had problems focusing on his paperwork for the rest of the day, his mind constantly coming back to S & G, Rust and the Apocalypse in waiting. So when Manny Povero called him up to see if he wanted to meet later for a drink with their friend, the writer Lee Jones, he accepted immediately. *Arts and literature always saved the day,* he thought, *as the Egregorians would have said.*

3

Le Robespierre was packed, but Ratner spotted the familiar faces of his two friends sitting at a table in the back. He had called Laura to see if she wanted to join them, but she had already made other dinner plans with a girlfriend from work.

Manny waved at him from afar while Ratner ordered his beer at the bar, and Lee Jones raised his glass.

"Short time no see," the writer said as Ratner sat down at their table.

"Always a pleasure," the Commissioner said. "What's up? Needed a break from the third wife?"

Lee shrugged and Manny laughed. "Exactly! My second wife, and his third! Thought we needed some man-time together . . ." the painter explained.

"You didn't say I couldn't invite Laura, though," Ratner remarked. "I actually called and asked her to join us, but she was busy somewhere else. Good thing, I guess."

Lee seemed to have drunk a few already, his glance shifting frequently to Ratner's face.

"You been here long?"

"No, we just arrived. Well, I just arrived," Manny answered. "I think Lee might have been here for a while."

"We love Laura," Lee said. "She's cool. She understands."

"Well, yes, she's very tolerant . . ." Ratner began.

"She understands the melancholy of this world," Lee resumed. "She understands that we're all going to die and that's why we should all mind our own business and let people be the way they want to be."

"Did you guys hear Delgado's speech last night?" Povero said, trying to change the conversation.

"No, what did she say?" Lee Jones asked.

Povero and Ratner exchanged a long glance and laughed. The painter explained what had happened the evening before in a few words.

The writer nodded, looking at his pint. "Bullshit," he said. "It's just to get re-elected. Then she'll go dancing with her banker friends again."

"Always the optimist," Povero said.

"Well, you read my books," Jones replied with a wink. "You *do* read my books, right?"

"Speaking of which," Ratner interjected. "I didn't have a chance to ask you last time—are you publishing anything soon?"

"Yeah, there's a novel coming this spring. I'll send you a copy when it's out." He stood up. "I need another beer."

Ratner watched the famous writer stagger to the bar. "He will never change," he said, remembering the young man Jones had been, ironic, dedicated, full of rage and alcohol.

"No, and I don't know if it's a good thing," Povero laughed. "Actually, it is. He is like a compass to us: keeps pointing in the same direction, while we meander to get where we want."

"Also keeps writing the same books, more or less. Sometimes I'm surprised by his success."

Povero played with his half-empty pint, watching the lights reflect on the glass. "Babylon is a masochist. It loves to be kicked in the balls, if the person kicking is famous. You know, like a court jester."

Lee Jones sat back down at the table, a fresh drink in hand. "Talking about me, I hope," he said jovially.

"Of course, what else?" Povero retorted. "And you, Georgie boy, what's up with you? You must be terribly busy now, being the top cop and all."

Ratner grunted and shrugged. "Yeah, it's kind of crazy these days, for sure."

"Remember when we were young and snotty?" Lee Jones said maliciously. "Man, who would have believed we'd all be part of the establishment thirty years later. It almost makes me want to cry."

Povero and Ratner hung their heads down, both as a joke and because they knew their writer friend was right.

"Better us than some other assholes," Povero finally said, raising his head again.

"Well said, my friend, well said!" Lee Jones approved noisily.

Ratner smiled and took a long sip of his beer. He felt warm inside and, to his surprise, almost happy.

"To us assholes," he joined in, raising his glass.

"No, no," Lee Jones corrected, putting a hand on his wrist. "To us *immortal* assholes!"

4

In the cab taking him home, Ratner heard on the radio that the trade unions had stopped the strike, but that Delgado and Rust were still extremely close in the polls. *Whatever,* Ratner mused, *we're all going to die sooner or later.* And he found the thought strangely comforting. Must have been Lee Jones's company that influenced him. Those writers; not surprising that governments and monsters wanted to kill them. They could even fucking undermine the fucking chief of the fucking police.

XX. JUDGMENT

Judgment: A sudden passion for free jazz. Thinking about joining a hippie community. Waking up to a cloudy day. Longing to see England again. Maybe it's time to start a family. Being loved by the world and being grateful for it.

1

Laura had made coffee before leaving for work and Ratner poured himself a cup. Looking through the window, he could imagine the traffic outside more than he actually saw it: a thick fog had descended upon Babylon, adorning the lights with strange halos and reducing the people to intermittent shadows. He thought about the Land of the Dead of the ancient stories and wondered if it looked like that. Maybe he would ask Nūt next time he saw her. The last three days had been a strange and unknown combination of stress and routine: routine in the paperwork and professional phone calls; stress from the general political climate and uncertainties.

Even if he wanted to remain as untouched as possible by politics, as city commissioner, everything he did, said, or didn't do or didn't say, had become political.

The fog outside was dense and heavy—neither beautiful nor ugly, just present, like a reminder of what reality really was: something that you walked through, not really seeing where you were going or the next thing you were going to bump into.

Lacroix had called him the previous night to tell him they had gathered enough evidence to officially launch the investigation into Green Star and its money laundering scheme. Ratner had in turn rung Flowers to set up a meeting for today—just the three of them: him, the DA and Lacroix.

This time he didn't want to blow up the whole city by himself. He had the match, he had the powder, but he didn't have the guts. Or rather, he didn't have the guts to do it alone. It was his age, probably. No more mavericking like in the good old days, when Valentino would sit next to him in the unmarked car, clenching his teeth while they sped through the city, wondering what was going to happen next and why the hell did they team him up with a complete lunatic?

Ratner smiled as he brought the hot mug to his lips. Poor Jesse Valentino, cop almost killed in action and famous unknown poet—quite an achievement, actually, in an ironical way. The man had remained on the margin both in life and death. He wondered if he was still walking in the fog out there, wherever he was now, if he was anywhere, or if everything was now crystal clear and incredibly sharp. Yes, he would definitely have to ask Nūt if the dead were as clueless as the living. Either way would make sense, as would an eternal and limitless night where nothing, absolutely nothing, ever happened.

2

Lacroix was already in the DA's office when Ratner walked in, his leather coat damp from the fog. DA Flowers asked him if he wanted some coffee, but Ratner turned the offer down.

"Just had a strong cup," he explained. "More java and my brain is going to send out blue sparks."

The two men were standing around the DA's desk, which drowned under a pile of binders Ratner recognized from the last meeting with his Finance Department colleague.

"I have a Powerpoint to explain everything," Lacroix said. "One moment, please."

He sat down, turned on his laptop and pushed a couple of keys. Figures and diagrams appeared on the screen. Lacroix did his best to explain the whole construction, which really was a genius money laundering scheme, as Ratner had surmised.

Green Star was indeed a front company buying coffee from shell charities that were themselves financed by cash coming from Green Star's main owner, S & G, through shell offshore companies S & G owned. It was a closed circuit, which not only washed dirty money, but also turned it into profit.

Lacroix explained that they had all the evidence they needed now to prosecute and bring down the whole financial setup. It would be an airtight case. They only needed the green light, he added, looking at Ratner and Flowers.

The DA nodded, pursing his lips. "I see," he said. "I see."

He rubbed his chin and stared at Ratner. "What do you think, Georg?"

"I think I know what you're thinking, Jim," Ratner answered. "That, at another time, this would be seen as fantastic police work—which it is—but that at this very moment, in this very particular situation, it's a fucking explosive device that can blow up everything."

Flowers nodded. "Yes, my thoughts, exactly."

Lacroix was puzzled. "I don't really understand," he said. "What's the problem? We've got all the evidence, my team worked its ass off for this."

Ratner sighed. "The problem, my dear Danny, is politics. You've done a great job, no question. But you see, I don't know if you've noticed, but we're right in the middle of an election race. And it happens that Green Star's CEO is Delgado's good buddy and that the guy who owns most of the shares in his company is Rust's son-in-law . . . We have to think carefully here. And I have to ask you a very personal question that has to remain between the four walls of this office—who do you support in this race? Delgado or Rust?"

"You can't ask him that!" Flowers objected. "It's personal!"

"I know, Jim, but we have a very important and delicate decision to make today, and I want to see all the players' hands. I can show you mine first: I don't like Delgado, but I would vote for her because I truly hate Rust and everything he stands for.

"DA Flowers officially supports Delgado, as we all know. So if you're in for Rust, Lacroix—which I respect, although you know where I stand now—we will have to take this into account in our discussion, and I might have to take you off the case—risking a political scandal on top of the coming political scandal. Do you understand? This is pure politics now, not police work anymore."

Lacroix nodded slowly, staring at all the files and the computer on the DA's desk.

"I understand totally," Lacroix said after a moment of silence. "And I am grateful for your honesty. I will vote for Delgado too, probably for the same reasons as you, City Commissioner. So, what do we do from here?"

Flowers looked at Ratner with visible relief, who grunted and shrugged. *Once a maverick, always a maverick*, he thought, refraining from smiling.

"Yes, Georg, what do we do?" Flowers asked.

"First, we sit down and yes, thank you, I will have some coffee now."

3

Sitting back behind his own desk, Ratner felt like a tired Roman senator at the time of Caesar. Everything was politics in this city, and some things more than others. He took out his cigarettes and lit one, enjoying the bitter flower opening within his lungs. He hadn't smoked all day, both Lacroix and Flowers being anti-tobacco fanatics. They had discussed the various possibilities over and over again, trying to find the most efficient and satisfying one, both legally and politically.

The case would be a long one. From the time they made the investigation public, to the various indictments and trials, months or perhaps years, would pass by.

The most important, for Flowers, was that Delgado would not be harmed by the investigation. Harding's suicide had to remain a suicide, and the origin of the investigation had to be an "anonymous tip," leaving Valentino out of it.

With Lacroix, they agreed to focus mainly on Blue Mist and the four other nonprofit organizations.

Flowers would tip off Back To Earth, who would conduct there own investigation, with the help of the documents discreetly provided by the DA's office, and make it a public case. Hopefully, Back To Earth would find out by themselves fairly soon who the CEO was behind the shell companies pouring dirty cash into the machine, thus leaving the DA's hands clean.

They also decided to leave Green Star out of it for now, at least until the election was over. If Delgado was re-elected, she would have no problem creating distance between her and a shady donor. If she didn't, then they would have something to attack the newly elected president with.

It wasn't clean, it wasn't nice, it wasn't satisfying, but Ratner didn't see any other option at the moment. If crime was a dirty business, then politics was sometimes dirtier, but at least you could fight crime frontally—it was never the case with politics.

Ratner took a long drag of his cigarette, reclining in his comfortable chair. He hoped Valentino and Harding would forgive him and understand that getting them justice, at least for now, had been sacrificed for a higher cause, even if it was a corrupt, despicable one.

4

"Did you have a good day at work?" Laura asked him as he walked into the living room.

He didn't answer immediately, but poured himself a double whisky, adding ice and water as usual.

"So, how was your day?" Laura asked him again, as he sat down next to her on the couch.

Rust was on the news, attacking the immigrants that, according to him, "lowered the democratic standards of the city, not to mention its intelligence." Ratner suddenly regretted not having launched a direct investigation against the bastard and drank a long golden sip.

"It's been a long day," he finally answered. "Not a bad day, not a good day, just a long, long day."

5

Valentino's ghost visited him in his dream. It was in Nūt's temple, but the goddess wasn't present. Ratner could only smell the trace of her perfume, which soothed his soul.

"I'm sorry about today, Jesse," he said. "There was nothing I could do."

The ghost answered nothing, just stood there, stars shining through its transparent shape, beautiful, cold and distant.

XXI. THE WORLD

The World: Enjoying the nice weather. Looking at yourself in the mirror and thinking you're not looking so bad after all. Thinking about starting a zoo. Writing a novel with both hands. Knowing that the outcome is near and that it will always be different than what you expect. Having a new neighbor that likes to walk around naked. Thinking of traveling by yourself.

1

"Allô? Yes?" Ratner waved Emma away. He couldn't think of her as Mrs. Gardiner anymore. She smiled as she shut the door behind her. He glanced at the files she had brought in. It was the Blue Mist investigation papers he had to sign. He focused back on what the voice on the phone was telling him.

"What? Really? I'll be there in a minute." He called his assigned driver feverishly.

They had caught Valentino's murderer. He couldn't believe it.

Maybe that was what Valentino's ghost had tried to let him know last night. And then again, maybe not.

2

A slender black woman in uniform welcomed him as he climbed up the steps of the northern district police station.

"Commissioner Millborne," she introduced herself as they shook hands. "The suspect is in the interrogation room. I thought you would want to be present when we begin the interview."

"Yes, of course. Thank you."

He followed the officer inside the large gray concrete building, his breath preceding him like a hopeful ghost.

3

Ratner observed the suspect through the one-way mirror glass. A scrubby guy, with a beard and crazy black and empty Charlie Manson eyes.

"He's a local junkie," Millborne explained. "We busted him for a failed burglary in a pharmacy, and we found this on him."

She held up an evidence bag that contained a wallet, a couple of sets of keys and what looked like Valentino's watch and notebook.

"One of the key sets matched your colleague's apartment, and the victim's name is inscribed on the notebook's first page," Millborne said, as she handed Ratner a pair of surgical gloves.

"The watch was his too," he said, extracting the notebook from the bag.

He hoped she didn't notice the slight trembling of his hands as he opened it. *Jesse Valentino* was indeed written on the first page, with his address underneath. He leafed rapidly through it. Poems, fragments, doodles. There was a title too: "In Praise of Night." *Couldn't be more prophetic*, Ratner thought sadly.

"What about Valentino's computer?" the city commissioner asked. "Did you find it?"

"No, it wasn't in the suspect's room."

Ratner nodded as he took out the wallet. He opened it. It was empty, except for the junkie's identification card and a few business cards: a strip club, a bar, a plumber, a Chinese takeaway. The last one made Ratner's eyebrows arch. It was Helena Gonzalez's card, all gold and creamy white.

"Did you see this?" he asked Millborne.

"Yeah. Strange. I wonder where he got that."

"Me too. For sure. Come on, let's go," he said.

"You're the boss, boss," Millborne said.

He smiled at her as she opened the connecting door to the interrogation room.

4

The junkie scratched his dirty black hair.

"I saw the watch. It looked expensive. So I followed him for a while and waited for the right moment. He stopped to buy a sandwich and that made him walk slower, because he was eating it. There was nobody around so I figured . . ."

Ratner nodded. "Then you got his keys, and you went into his apartment. What did you find there?"

"Stuff," the junkie sniffled. "You know."

"Like a computer?" Ratner asked.

The man nodded, caressing his yellowish cheeks.

"What did you do with it?," Millborne asked. "It wasn't in your room."

"I threw it away. In the river, to be exact."

"Why?" Ratner asked, surprised.

"Well, I turned it on and there was this code I needed to type in and stuff. Too complicated. I knew I could never sell it. And as I had killed a cop, it would have been too hot to handle anyway. It was a dead weight, so I got rid of it."

"Where? Can you tell us precisely where?" Ratner asked as Millborne was taking notes.

"Nah, I don't remember. It was night and I was on the stuff. You know how it is when you're high, can't think clearly."

"You mean you went all the way to the river to get rid of it? That's a long subway ride, Andy."

"Yeah, it was," the junkie said, nodding as if it made his statement more convincing.

"What about this?" Ratner asked again, showing the suspect Gonzalez's card. "Where did you get this?"

The junkie stared at the rectangular piece of expensive cardboard as if he had seen it for the first time. "Dunno. Must have found it somewhere."

"Hmm," Ratner said. "Why did you keep it?"

"Dunno. It's pretty, I think. And maybe I would need a lawyer. It's a good card to have."

"I doubt Miss Gonzalez would represent you," Millborne said.

The junkie looked at her defiantly. "Oh yeah? Well, you might be surprised. Very surprised."

"One last thing," Ratner said. "There was a notebook. With poems in it. Why did you keep that?"

The junkie shrugged. "I took it with the rest, you know. Then later I opened it and read some of the stuff. It was good. So I kept it. I actually read the whole thing twice."

Ratner had heard enough and signaled Millborne the interrogation was over for him.

Leaving the building, he turned toward the captain. "Try to push him more over Gonzalez," he said. "There is something very fishy about this."

"Yes, sir. My thoughts exactly."

"Keep me posted. You did a great job."

"Thank you, sir."

Climbing carefully down the icy steps Ratner thought about Shakr Bassam and the whole crazy conspiracy theory. It didn't seem completely crazy now, and he wondered what an égrégore actually looked like.

5

"Hello Ali, sorry to call you up at this time, but I've got some news about Valentino's murder."

Ratner suddenly wondered if his private cell phone was tapped and what the Secret Service would think about his crazy conversations with a high-ranking cop from Samarqand. He also wondered if Valentino had been about to become an infiltrated Samarqandi agent, maybe even manipulated by Bassam himself.

"Yes, don't worry. I'm listening, dear Georg."

Ratner filled him in on the arrest and the curious presence of Gonzalez's business card.

"Ah, ah," Bassam said. "Very interesting indeed. I gather this lawyer has political connections, yes? In any case, I would really protect that witness, if I were you. He could be a big problem for our égrégore . . ."

Ratner thanked Bassam for his advice and hung up. He looked at his watch and picked up his office phone. "Captain Millborne? Commissioner Ratner. I just had a thought. I don't like that Gonzalez card in our suspect's wallet. Can you put him in isolation and make sure nothing happens to him? Thanks."

Emma knocked on the door and walked in with a new stack of files crowding her arms.

"There you go, Georg. More fascinating papers for you to look at," she said as she dropped the load on his desk.

He sighed as he stared at the huge piles in front of him, then took the first file on the top of the left column. It was a completely random choice, but it could also be considered a method: dealing with the absurd through the absurd.

6

In the restaurant later that evening, Laura asked him again if they could have a cat. Ratner got annoyed because he thought this discussion was finished.

"No," he said. "Period."

"But why?" Laura asked, dipping her sushi roll into the soy sauce.

"Because who would take care of it when we go traveling?"

"We never go traveling," she said, pouting. "You're always too busy."

"Well, we do go out on weekends sometimes," he protested.

"Yes, twice in three years. I am sure we can find someone to feed it for two or three days."

Ratner's cell phone suddenly rang, saving him from what in his mind was a useless discussion. He frowned as he heard the news. "Very well, thank you. Keep me posted."

"Shit," he said as he put the phone in his pocket.

"What's wrong, baby?" Laura asked, worried.

"Nothing. It's just bad news from work."

The dealer had hung himself with his T-shirt in his cell. Or at least, that was what it looked like, Millborne had said.

So predictable, he thought. *So fucking, fucking predictable.*

He sighed and carefully drank some of his very hot jasmine tea.

"Okay, we can get a cat," he finally said.

Sometimes, only the unpredictable could save you. That's where your freedom lay. And the last refuge of your sanity.

XXII/0. THE FOOL

The Fool: Creative inspiration. Leaving home for no reason whatsoever. A possibility of peace through ignorance. Stepping in dog shit. Immunity against poison. Coming home for no reason whatsoever.

1

Weeks had gone by, then a month, before Ratner finally got the envelope he had been waiting for. Delgado had been re-elected to everyone's surprise, by a small 12,000 vote margin. Rust had called foul play and wanted the votes recounted. He was now waiting for a City Court decision to know whether his complaint had been accepted. Delgado's desperate populist strategy had apparently worked.

Now everybody was waiting for the changes, him included. It would be nice to have more personnel and fewer overworked hours.

The Blue Mist investigation, as the media called it, was going its course, sending waves of panic around S & G and the Rust family.

Opening the thin envelope on his dining table, Ratner felt once again his fingers tremble slightly as they took hold of Valentino's notebook. As Valentino had no family, he had asked Millborne if she could do him a last favor and send him the notebook when all the paperwork was done. It had taken more than a month, but here it was, finally. Sitting next to his chair, Ramses, the kitten, was watching him with his strange blue eyes, and Ratner gently patted the curious beastling on the head.

He opened the notebook and began to read some of the poems, while Valentino's ghost sat on the other side of the table, all mysteriously silent and transparent.

2

"Here, I think you guys should have it," Ratner said, handing Valentino's notebook to Doug Hale.

The bookseller carefully took the object and caressed its cover. "Thank you so very much, Commissioner," Hale said. "It will be very well taken care of, I can guarantee you that."

Ratner smiled, a little embarrassed. "I hope this will help you in your fight against those evil monsters," he half-joked.

"Yes, it will. And if you ever want to join us, you will be most welcome. I talked about it with Bassam. He agrees. We need people like you among us."

The city commissioner nodded. "I will think about it. Promise."

Leaving the shop, he turned around one last time. The Magic Mountain looked as it did the first time he had been there: discreet, unimpressive and possibly eternal.

3

When he got back his office after his quick lunch break visit to the Egregorians' bookstore, he saw Captain Eris Jordan waiting for him, as well as two men dressed in suits. They both reeked of Secret Service, especially because their shoes were so polished they reflected the white neon light shining above.

"Georg, these people are waiting for you," Emma said, stating the obvious.

He greeted them and they all stepped into his office. Emma brought an extra chair from the corridor, which Captain Jordan sat on.

"It's about that Synth situation, sir," Captain Jordan said. "These gentlemen have some info about that Vita woman."

One of the men, a young man with a 1950s part in his hair, produced a laptop from his satchel and put it on Georg's desk.

"I think you should see this, sir," he said. "Thanks to your identikit and other tips, we have finally managed to trace the suspect's lodgings. You have to know that we were aware of her existence before your investigation, and that we have only decided to inform you of our progress because there might have occurred unwanted interference between our respective departments."

"The Secret Service is investigating Synth too?" Ratner asked, only half-surprised, as he knew it had become a national cause during the elections.

The second man—older, with a completely bald head and buttonhole black eyes—said nothing but turned on the computer. A CCTV image appeared on the screen. He paused the image.

"As I was saying, we learned of the suspect's address and decided to put up a combined operation with your services. Captain Eris here was present," the first man explained.

"Why wasn't I informed?" Ratner asked, miffed.

"It was top secret," the second man said. He had a lisp, which contrasted strangely with his tough appearance. "We couldn't take the risk of any leaks. We didn't even tell Captain Eris what the real mission was—we said we were targeting a Synth lab—"

"—and this is what happened," the first man interrupted, pointing at the screen.

The images showed both police and unmarked cars parking in front of a nondescript brick building.

"East District, by the harbor?" Ratner asked.

"Yes, sir," the first man said.

Uniformed cops and plainclothes officers blocked the street while others rushed inside.

The second man clicked the forward symbol. The cops came out of the building, carrying boxes. It went on for a while, then they got back in their cars and left. A few plain clothes remained near the entrance of the building.

"No suspect arrested? She wasn't there?" Ratner asked, puzzled. "Had she been warned?"

"That's what we thought," the first man answered. "We found all these boxes filled with Synth pills, but no, she wasn't there. And she should have been. Our informers had seen her go inside the building and all the exits were monitored. But . . . nothing."

"That is strange," Ratner said. "Very strange."

"Wait," the first man said, clicking the forward symbol again. "It gets weirder."

The last plainclothes officer left. The street was empty, until suddenly a pair of legs materialized out of nowhere on the sidewalk, then a whole body. It was Vita, hurrying away with a little black backpack on her shoulders.

"Wait, what?" Ratner said.

"Exactly what we said too," the second man said.

"How is that possible?" Ratner asked again.

"Look closely. I'm going to play it in slow motion and enlarge the image."

It was as if a curtain slowly lifted upward from the heels of the woman. Slowly, slowly her whole body appeared as if a blanket or a drape was being pulled.

"An invisibility cape?" Ratner asked, hearing the absurdity of his own words. "Do they exist?"

The second man shrugged.

"We don't know what it is," the first man said, shutting his laptop. "Really advanced technology, in any case. She might work for a hostile city-state that might have developed such a device. But it's only speculation. So this is a question of national security now. From this point forward, you must share every bit of information you come up with during your investigations on Synth with us."

The second man produced a document from the inside pocket of his jacket. "It's all written down here. Express orders," he said. "Signed by President Delgado herself."

Ratner stared first at the piece of official paper, then at Captain Jordan, who shrugged discreetly. "Very well, gentlemen, you can count on me."

They left with only a nod—no handshake, no goodbye, no polite and professional formula.

"I'm very sorry I didn't contact you about the operation, sir," Captain Jordan apologized. "But they put a lot of pressure on me."

"It's fine, Captain. You did well. But whatever you find on Synth from now on, it's me first, Okay?"

Captain Jordan nodded vigorously and left.

Ratner looked at the closed door and let out a sigh. This world was becoming pure madness, and it wasn't even that funny anymore. *I am either getting too old for the circus*, he thought, *or I just realized that I am myself an elephant.*

4

In the car driving him home, Ratner asked the driver to switch on the radio. A familiar tune filled the car.

"Plus Equals Minus," he said out loud.

"You know them, sir?" the officer behind the wheel asked, surprised.

Ratner looked at the cop, a young Asian man with a constellation of pimples.

"Of course I know them. Love their stuff. Even met them once," he added, enjoying the look of awe in the officer's eyes.

5

Ramses ran toward Georg as he stepped into the apartment, and rubbed its minute white and gray body against the commissioner's legs.

"Glad to see you too," Ratner said, lifting the fur ball with one hand.

The kitten meowed weakly, making Georg laugh. He hated to admit it, but Laura had been right on this one. And Nūt too, about unsatisfactory solutions always being the ones that maintained balance in this world.

The kitten meowed again and Georg put it gently down on the ground.

"What do you know about politics, Ramses?" he asked the cat as he poured some milk in a bowl.

The kitten meowed its complete ignorance on the subject and ran to the bowl, licking the milk with feline enthusiasm.

Ratner poured himself a whisky and turned the TV on. He switched the channels until he found a documentary on early China.

"Who needs to travel," he said out loud to the cat while sipping his cold whisky, "when you have 147 TV channels, offering you both the entire knowledge and the utter stupidity of this world?"

As if to demonstrate complete agreement, Ramses sat down and began to lick its tiny asshole.

About the Author

Seb Doubinsky is a bilingual writer born in Paris in 1963. His novels, all set in a dystopian universe revolving around competing city-states, have been published in the UK and in the USA, and translated into numerous languages. He currently lives with his family in Aarhus, Denmark, where he teaches at the university.